RUM PUNCH
AND PREJUDICE

To: Luther & Peter,
With Love,

Caglan
Sep-28/98

RUM PUNCH
AND PREJUDICE

RAGLAN RIVIERE

JANUS PUBLISHING COMPANY
London, England

First published in Great Britain 1998
by Janus Publishing Company Limited,
Edinburgh House, 19 Nassau Street,
London W1N 7RE

www.januspublishing.co.uk

**A CIP catalogue record for this book
is available from the British Library.**

ISBN 1 85756 319 0

Phototypeset in 11 on 13 Goudy Old Style
by Keyboard Services, Luton, Beds

Cover design John Anastasio – Creative Line

Printed and bound in Great Britain by
Antony Rowe Ltd, Chippenham, Wiltshire

To Denise, my wife and best friend, whose patience and ongoing encouragement loom large in the production of this work. Thank you, my love.

CHAPTER ONE

BRUCE KNOWLES stirred beneath the blanket when the metallic rapping of the door flap invaded his sleep. The mail had arrived. He grimaced, yawned, turned to one side, then peered at his wristwatch. Eleven o'clock. He mumbled in disgust, then rose to hurry to the bathroom.

It was a warm day in May 1960 in the borough of Lambeth, London, England. The hum of the traffic forced its way through the open bathroom window, while the sun fought a losing battle in its attempt to crack the misty haze. Bruce yawned once more and was staggering back to bed when the brightly coloured envelopes on the first-floor landing caught his attention. He descended the stairs.

Bruce had just completed night work and had slept barely three hours. He wobbled slightly while stooping to gather the letters from the floor and immediately his eyes focused on the air-mail envelope displaying vivid red and blue stripes. When he noticed 'Dominica' on the stamp a sudden chill crept through his body. 'My God,' he exclaimed, 'it's uncle Henry!' He turned the envelope and read, 'Clifford A. Johnson, Chambers.' Hurriedly, Bruce opened the envelope and began reading while climbing the stairs. He dropped the other letters on the bedside table and sat gently on the edge of the bed. With eyes glued to his reading, he transferred the letter to his left hand and cradled his chin in the right. His head lowered to his chest and remained there till he finished. Slowly, he lifted his head, dropping the letter on the bed. He was wide awake now.

The house was quiet. Betty, his wife, was at work in Clapham and Sandra, his daughter and only child, was at school. Bruce could turn only to his pipe for company. Carefully, he dug out the charred tobacco from his last smoke and tenderly refilled the pipe with fresh moist and golden shreds. He eased back against the headboard, pulled the blanket over his legs, then sucked twice on the unlit pipe to test the air flow. He reached for the box of matches on the bedside table, cracked a match and gazed briefly at the dancing flame before lighting his pipe.

The furrowed tension on his brow melted away magically as he inhaled. The room filled with a sweet aroma of tobacco. He glanced at the letter beside him, fingered it gently, then smiled at the thought which it had brought to his mind. 'In my twelve years with British Railways I have never done managerial work. How could I be expected to manage a large estate like Riversdale Plantations?' He laughed at the seeming absurdity of it all. But his derision was brief and hollow, since he was faced with a very serious proposition and with only two weeks in which to decide.

Bruce breathed deeply, let out a long heavy sigh, then closed his eyes in contemplation. From the letter, it was clear that his uncle was seriously ill and was unable to continue to manage the plantations. Bruce would become heir to the estate, but only on condition that he would continue in the tradition of his father Charles and uncle Henry. Bruce had shown no interest in Riversdale Plantations, especially from the time his father died. Consequently, his uncle was prepared to donate the plantations to the people of Dominica for experimental purposes if Bruce declined the offer.

'What did I get from them, anyway?' Bruce murmured. 'Why should they put me in this awkward position now?' His bitterness was reflected in the coarse tone of his voice. 'If they love the natives of Dominica more than their own flesh and blood then let the blacks have Riversdale!' The saliva in the stem of the pipe croaked when Bruce sucked once more. The tobacco was drowned. The pipe turned cold. Bruce was angry.

Sandra closed the front door heavily behind her and headed straight for the kitchen. She was hungry. She dropped her school

[2]

bag on the floor, turned on the television, and opened the refrigerator, all in one well rehearsed movement.

Upstairs, Bruce rolled onto his back, still clutching the letter in his left hand and continued to snore in defiance of his daughter's interruptions below.

Sandra gulped a mouthful of cold milk to facilitate the swallowing of biscuit and cheese. When advertisements came on, Sandra scurried up to the bathroom, climbing two steps at a time.

'Is that you, Sandra?' Her father shouted from the bedroom, clearly annoyed at being woken up by the noise.

'Yes, dad,' Sandra shouted a muffled response from the bathroom.

'Okay, keep the noise down, will you?' Bruce begged, turning once more to his side.

'Sorry, dad,' Sandra apologised as she hurried stealthily back down to the television. She sat heavily on the armchair, bent to reach her shoelaces and soon shoes and socks were thrown on the floor beside her school bag. In a matter of minutes the quiet order of the kitchen-diner was transformed into noisy disarray.

Bruce was wide awake once more; his snoring had conceded defeat to Sandra's laughter and the television. He got out of bed, stretched his arms above his head, yawning audibly. He donned his bathrobe and staggered to the bathroom.

Sandra's favourite programme ended. She gathered her belongings off the floor and went to her room, forgetting to turn off the television. No sooner had she changed her clothes than the key turned open the front door signalling Betty's return from work.

'Hi mom,' Sandra shouted from upstairs.

'Hello, dear. How was school?' her mother inquired.

'Okay,' Sandra replied without much enthusiasm as she walked down to greet her mother.

'Is your father awake?'

'Yes, I'm awake,' Bruce replied softly, appearing at the top of the stairs. 'Sandra made sure of that. And I've got some very interesting news for you.' His tone showed no emotion.

'It had better be good,' Betty commented. 'I had a rough day.'

They greeted each other with a kiss and entered the kitchen where Betty immediately began to prepare the afternoon tea. This was a ritual for the family, huddling before the television while sharing their day's activities over a cup of tea.

'I don't know if I should call it good or bad news,' Bruce voiced after some thought, 'but it's all in this letter.' He placed the letter on the coffee table nearest to Betty's usual seat.

'May I see it, dad?' Sandra was curious.

'Sure, go ahead. This involves you too.'

'Me!' Sandra exclaimed, grabbing the letter anxiously.

Bruce sighed heavily as he stretched his arms and legs in an effort to find a more comfortable position on the old chesterfield. 'Pardon me,' he begged, 'I haven't slept a wink.'

'Well, you're on days off now, aren't you?' Betty enquired.

'Hm,' Bruce grunted affirmatively.

There was sudden quietness in the kitchen when the whistling kettle was turned off. Betty poured the boiling water into the teapot and carefully carried the loaded tray to the coffee table.

With eyes wide open, lips parted, Sandra continued to read avidly. Her expression clearly revealed the interesting nature of the news.

'Not finished yet?' Betty asked impatiently. But, Sandra did not hear her mother, for her thoughts were far away on an island she had heard of but did not know. 'Guess it must be good news, after all.' Betty turned her attention to pouring the tea. 'Who is it from?' She asked her husband finally.

'Uncle Henry's solicitor in Dominica,' Bruce answered casually.

'What's happened?' Betty's mild curiosity turned into anxiety.

'They are asking me to return to take over the management of the estate, because uncle Henry is very ill.'

'Oh dear!' Betty sighed sorrowfully.

Bruce slurped some tea, then continued. 'It is uncle's dying wish for me to continue the tradition of the family,' he paused for another sip, 'or else the estate will be given to the people of Dominica.'

'To the people?' Betty's mood changed dramatically. 'Is this for estate duty, or are they turning communist, like Africa, and taking over white people's property?'

Bruce smiled at his wife's vivid imagination. 'Oh, I don't know, but I guess not, because the estate will be used for experiments.'

'It's a blooming shame, though, that after so many years of hard work your father and uncle Henry put into building the estate, to give the whole thing away for nothing.' Betty always placed great value on hard work. She often recalled for Sandra's benefit the hard, labouring days of her youth in the north of England.

'How much is the estate worth, dad?' Sandra passed the letter to her mother who began reading anxiously.

'I don't know, San,' Bruce raised his eyebrows as if to wonder, 'but, tens of thousands of pounds I imagine.'

'Great Scott!' Sandra exclaimed in awe.

'I remember we had four hundred acres when I was a boy.' Bruce smiled with pride at the memory. 'Who knows, maybe it's more or less today.'

'Four hundred acres!' Sandra echoed, trying to imagine the size. 'That's huge!'

'It certainly was in those days,' Bruce began to reminisce. 'We were like lords then. Everybody looked up to us, because we were very rich and hundreds of people depended on us for their living.' He stopped abruptly as unpleasant memories came rushing in. 'Oh, well, those were the good old days,' he concluded.

'Are we going back?' Sandra asked with unabashed relish at the prospect. There was a lively glimmer in her eyes as she waited on her father's response with childish expectancy.

Bruce smiled a grunt. 'Hm, I don't know. It's been a long time, San, twenty-five years to be exact, since I left the island. I've never been back.'

'What's it like there dad? What are the people like? Is the weather always sunny, and are there lots of sandy beaches?'

'I really can't tell now, San. There must have been quite a few changes. I was just fifteen when I left.'

Her father's reluctance to talk about the island smothered Sandra's curiosity, leaving her emotionally suspended. 'You don't like it do you, dad?' She was direct as children will be to those they trust.

'To be frank, not very much.'

'Why not?' Sandra probed.

'All right, Sandra!' Betty intervened. 'Daddy doesn't want to talk about this now.' She knew only too well what bitter memories her husband held of the island and wanted to spare him the ordeal.

'Some other time, San, I will tell you all I can remember about Dominica, and in particular why I am not fond of it.' He paused, then added, 'Not as a home, anyway.'

Sandra's face drooped with disappointment. She turned towards the television as if to cut herself away from her parents. Betty and Bruce eyed each other in the uneasy silence which followed, then sipped tea in harmony.

'Four hundred acres is a lot to give up, Bruce.' Betty broke the silence, being overwhelmed by the magnitude of the estate.

Bruce sensed what was to follow. He knew Betty had always wanted to visit the place of his birth on vacation. He had always resisted. But, now, the ideal opportunity was presenting itself.

'It would be nice to give it a trial before saying no,' she suggested.

Sandra's face lit up, eyes aglow, ears pricked. She abandoned the television for the imminent confrontation between her parents.

Bruce remained silent, yet pensive. He never made decisions without consulting Betty. He had already told her why he did not want to return to the island. He had also written his uncle explaining why he refused to return to attend his father's funeral. His wounds were deep.

'You know, Bruce,' Betty was nodding her head as she spoke, 'a lot of water has passed under the bridge since you left Dominica.'

Sandra smiled at this quaint saying and added, 'And, times change, and so do men.'

Bruce looked at his wife and daughter, then laughed. 'You two talk as if I have already decided to reject the invitation.' He was taken aback by his own words and added cautiously, 'but, nor have I decided to accept.'

Betty saw a glimmer of hope. She, like Sandra, loved change, new places, new friends, new challenges. They had visited every coastal resort in the south of England, but had never left its shores. Bruce, on the other hand, sought stability and security, which Betty saw as stagnation. 'I guess we will have to do some serious thinking about this,' Betty concluded. She gathered the cups onto the tray then stepped into the kitchen.

Sandra turned her attention fully to the television while Bruce found solace in his pipe. Relaxed by the sweet aroma, Bruce's thoughts took wings to the island of his birth. He let them dwell on the memory of his mother's death. Twelve years of age at the time, he remembers sitting at her bedside, with aunt Maria, uncle Henry's wife. He knew his mother was dying but could not understand why.

His mother was lying helplessly on her back, propped up by several pillows. Her mouth remained open, her face twisted in agony. She was gasping for breath as if each were her last. Then Bruce remembered that brief, but joyful, moment when his mother had smiled faintly as he touched her hand. His tears came easily, then, for there was hope. He had prayed shamelessly, asking God to let her get well. But her gasping became more difficult. Then, when aunt Maria was taking him out of the room his mother exhaled a long, heavy, raspy breath. He looked back to see his mother's face regain its calmness and tranquillity. She had joined the angels in Heaven, he thought.

He remembered the loneliness he felt at the loss of the one he loved the most. His father, Charles, was too busy at the estate. Margaret, the housekeeper, was no substitute for his mother. Furthermore, he resented the way she would smile at his father. He hated it, too, when his father would put his arms around her the way he used to hold his mother.

But Bruce will never forget the sharp pain which pierced his heart that afternoon when he returned home early after the Inspector of Schools had granted a half day holiday following a visit to his school. He was looking forward to joining his father on the estate. He had rushed into the bedroom to change his clothes when, to his horror, right before his very eyes, on the bed which his mother had shared with his father, Margaret and his father were locked in love's embrace.

'Oh damn!' Bruce blurted out as he jolted himself back to the present.

'Pardon me, dad?' Sandra asked, believing that her father was commenting on the television show.

'I was just thinking aloud.' Bruce rose from his seat, walked with deliberate slowness up the stairs to join Betty. He stopped briefly at the bedroom door, looked at the letter in his hand, then opened the door and said, 'Let's give it a try, love, eh? What do you say?'

Betty looked at him with confused amazement. Waves of happiness bathed her body. She stood speechless for a while, then heard herself say, 'I'm all for it, love, if you are.' She dropped the hair brush on the bed to embrace her husband warmly. Yet, her alert sixth sense signalled caution. 'Are you sure? Maybe we should talk some more about it.'

'The way I see it, Betty, we have nothing to lose by trying. You are right. It is better to have tried and failed than not to try and wonder later what we might have gained.' Bruce sat heavily on the bed as if exhausted from intense deliberation. 'Besides, I am the legal heir to Riversdale Plantations. I would hate to see my father's hard-earned wealth fall into the hands of ignorant blacks.

'Good Lord, Bruce! When will you change these gross feelings for these people?' Betty was always disturbed by her husband's less than charitable attitude towards blacks. 'How can you feel this way about them and at the same time want to live among them?'

'Betty, we won't have to live with them.' Bruce assumed a defensive posture. 'Over there we are the masters and they are the servants. That is the way it is, and that is the way it will always be!'

Betty had heard this speech before. But she could not understand what manner of ignorance motivated blacks in England to own businesses, houses, cars, hold very good jobs both in government and industry, and fill the universities. She thought of her black co-workers whom she found very friendly but by no means ignorant. One of her supervisors was black, well-liked and as efficient as any white counterpart. 'Maybe it would be a mistake to return to the island, Bruce.'

Bruce smiled. He understood what Betty was saying. 'Do not worry, love,' he reassured her, 'I have no intentions of destroying the reputation my father and uncle built over the years. If we find the conditions intolerable, then we will return to good old England. Is that a deal?' He smiled teasingly.

Betty embraced him once more. 'That is definitely good news! Let's tell San!'

CHAPTER TWO

L IKE A sentinel guarding the entrance to the Roseau valley, Knowles Gardens spread for two acres at the neck of the Woodbridge estuary. Flanked by towering coconut and grugru palms on the east and west, the winding, lazy river on the north, and an access road surfaced with tarrish on the south, the home of the Knowles family enjoyed an enviable reputation for horticultural excellence. It has been the venue of several fund-raising socials for charitable purposes, visited by tourists and horticulturalists around the world, and frequently graced by the visits of His Honour, the Administrator.

Today, however, a cloud of sadness overshadowed the home. Henry Knowles was dying. Mable Prince, the housekeeper, had been crying for several days now which made it increasingly difficult for her to attend to the unending procession of friends and well-wishers. Mable had been a domestic worker with the Knowles family since she was fifteen. Now, at forty-eight, she was like one of them, loved and respected by all.

Clifford Johnson pulled into the driveway and parked. With briefcase in hand he entered the hallway without knocking.

'Oh, Mr Clifford, good mornin'.' Mable could not conceal her anxiety. 'I fink we should call Fadder Patrick, quick! Mr Henry look bad, bad, bad today! He not drinkin' his soup, an' he not sayin' noffing!'

'Is Dr Korbinsky here yet?' Clifford was more concerned about health than death. As solicitor and confidant to the Knowles family he had grown very fond of Henry and would want the best for him.

'Yes Mr Clifford; he an' nurse inside wif Mr Henry.'

Clifford placed his hand on Mable's shoulder and smiled reassuringly. 'God is good, Mable. He takes care of all those who love Him. Right now He is taking care of Henry.' He smiled again, then entered the corridor leading to Henry's room.

'You right, Mr Clifford,' Mable murmured to herself. 'God know what He doin', jus' to believe in Him an' everyfing will be awright.' Mable always found peace in her faith. With this prayer she braced herself to face and accept God's will.

Henry Knowles lay motionless on the bed, head and back supported by pillows. Nurse Beatrice Andrews was assisting Dr Korbinsky in setting up the intravenous apparatus. 'How is he, doc?' Clifford was soft spoken.

'Not too good. Too weak to swallow so we are mounting this feeding drip.' Dr Korbinsky was blunt when he added, 'Just a matter of time now. The affliction has long past its threshold. Henry is still with us purely by the strength of his will.'

'And by the grace of God,' Clifford added.

Dr Korbinsky bled the tubes and inserted the needle into Henry's right arm. Nurse Andrews stabilised the arm and tubes while the doctor updated the record on Henry's medical chart.

'Well, that's it for now, Cliff,' Dr Korbinsky concluded. 'In about two hours Henry may be strong enough to whisper.' Then, touching Henry on his shoulder, he leaned towards his left ear and said, 'I'll be back this evening, Henry. Don't exert yourself, whatever you do.'

'Did he hear you?' Clifford asked curiously.

'He should have, but his senses are severely dulled. They will improve as he regains strength, I mean … if he does.' Dr Korbinsky was cautiously hopeful.

'I guess I'll have to speak with him later.' Clifford opened the door for the doctor following closely behind.

From the living room Eugene St Rose watched the two men with briefcases approaching. These were the two most influential men on the island, he was thinking. Clifford Johnson, the English lawyer, most people feared; but why he never could

[12]

understand, since he had represented so many people without fee who would otherwise face the courts without benefit of counsel. Henry Korbinsky was a well-loved and respected Polish doctor. This was understandable because doctors are revered like little gods who save lives. Their presence together at the residence of Henry Knowles was testimony enough of Knowles' high standing on the island.

'Ah, Eugene,' Clifford recognised the overseer of Riversdale Plantations. 'I'm glad I met you.' Turning, he bade farewell to Dr Korbinsky, then greeted Eugene with a gentle pat on the shoulder. Eugene smiled sheepishly, his white teeth sparkling against his ebony face. 'I would like to discuss the future of Riversdale with you and Samuel,' Clifford continued. 'Shall we meet here in Henry's office tomorrow at two?'

'Of course, Mr Johnson,' Eugene confirmed. 'I was meaning to ask you about it seeing that Mr Knowles is so, well, you know, very sick and all that.'

'Well, ma boy,' Clifford used this habitual phrase whenever he addressed a subordinate. 'The king is dead, long live the king!' Clifford kept nodding his head as if he was only now realising the significance of what he said.

'I don't understand you, sir.'

'Bruce Knowles, Henry's nephew and son of Charles, is returning from England to take over from Henry.' Clifford chuckled at the turn of events, then proceeded, 'Bruce was sent to England some twenty-five years ago for schooling. He has not been back since.' He paused once more, shaking his head in disbelief, then in a sombre tone he said, 'But, Henry felt it only fair to offer him the estate, if he wanted it.'

'I see.' Eugene aped Clifford's nodding.

'Yes, and that's why I want you and Samuel, and perhaps Mable, to discuss plans to receive our new master.' He slapped Eugene's shoulder in friendly gesture. 'So, we shall see tomorrow.'

'Awright, Mr Johnson.' Eugene, still bewildered by the news, gazed at the open doorway for some time after Clifford left. 'Bruce Knowles,' he murmured. 'Never once heard his name mentioned. Didn't even know Charles Knowles had a son.'

[13]

Eugene remembered why he had come to Knowles Gardens. He, too, was concerned about the future of Riversdale with the impending death of Henry Knowles. He turned towards the kitchen just when Mable was approaching him with a beautiful, beaming smile.

'Hello, Eugie, is good to see you.' Mable loved him as the son she longed for but never had.

'Hi, Mabes,' Eugene greeted. 'How is Mr Knowles?'

'Not good at all, Eugie, not good at all.' Mable was almost in tears.

'Well, Mabes, the Lord giveth and the Lord taketh away. The old must make way for the new.' Eugene embraced her warmly, then asked, 'Did you know his brother's son Bruce?'

'If I know Brucie! Boy, I cry so much when dey sen' him away. Dey didn' like him,' Mable recalled with a note of disapproval in her voice.

'Who didn't like him? And why they didn't like him?' Eugene's interest was aroused.

'Dat bitch, Margaret! Lord, forgive me! You rem'ber Margaret, de housekeeper?' Mable turned bitter.

'Yes, I do. She left when Charles died,' Eugene recalled.

'Dat's right. She go *because* Mr Charles die. But nobody wouldn' want her to stay.' Mable paused to compose herself. 'You see, Mr Charles use to make fun wif her, but, she let it go to her head an' so she forget her place in de house.'

'So what about Bruce?' Eugene egged on.

'Well, would you believe, as soon as Miss Bella die, Margaret fin' herself in Miss Bella bed wif Mr Charles? Oh Lord, God! An' would you know, Brucie come from school an' fin' dem in his mama bed! Lord, have mercy! An' dat is why Brucie hate his papa an' Margaret so.' Mable raised both hands high in supplication to her God.

'Is that why they sent him to England?'

'Dey say is for school, but I know better, because Brucie didn' want to go. De day he see dem in his mama bed Brucie run away. But, I fin' him by de river near de water pipe, cryin'. Brucie tell me all what happen an' from den I was like his mama.'

[14]

'Well, Mabes, Bruce is coming back.'

'Brucie comin' home?' She repeated excitedly. Eugene smiled at the sudden transformation of Mable's countenance from sadness to perplexity. Then, she observed sadly, 'So he comin' for his uncle funeral, but he never come when his own fadder die.' Mable's voice broke with remorse.

'He is coming back to stay, Mabes. He is going to be the new master of Knowles Gardens.'

Mable was speechless as she stood staring at Eugene. 'Well, bless dis house, oh Lord!' She finally exclaimed clapping her hands, truly overjoyed by the news.

'Tomorrow, Mr Johnson will be coming here to speak with us about this, so keep it a secret.' Eugene felt her joy which was the more pronounced against the backdrop of the imminent death of Henry Knowles.

'Awright, Eugie, an' fanks for de good news.'

'You are so fortunate, Betty,' Simone said with a hint of jealousy. 'I wish I could be going to the Caribbean to get away from those dreadful London winters. How romantic it must be with sunshine and sandy beaches all year round.' Simone sighed in her fantasy.

'I have no idea, Simone,' Betty remarked, 'but, I'll soon find out.'

'I would love to lie on the beach, sipping rum and coconut water, and dancing to the calypso and mambo.' Simone wiggled her body erotically to the imagined beat, spilling some of her gin and tonic in the process. 'Oops! I'm sorry,' she cried out, ending in laughter as the other guests were entertained by her theatricals.

There were about thirty people at the farewell party, close friends of Betty and Bruce. Like a rugby scrum, the men huddled together, holding mugs of ale and exchanging frivolities. Bruce was not quite prepared for the question Andrew St Claire had asked him. Others in the group took the question lightly, exploding with laughter. But, not so Andrew St Claire.

'I am quite serious, Bruce,' Andrew insisted after the laughter subsided. 'I know you well enough now. You have told me how much you hate these blacks. So I'm just asking why would you want to live in a black man's country?' There was no laughter now. The silence brought a hot flash to Bruce's face.

'You know, Andrew,' Bruce smiled, 'I hate the guts of quite a few white Englishmen, yet I live in England.' A murmur of approval was heard from some guests, which broadened Bruce's smile.

'Come now, Bruce, that's different, and you know it,' Andrew dismissed with a wave of the hand. 'You don't hate the white race, but there is no denying, you hate the black man because he is black!' Andrew's outspoken remarks in the company of others were possible only because of his close friendship with Bruce. Bruce regarded Andrew as his older brother. They were drinking partners, belonged to the same cricket club, and worked in the same department at British Railways. But Andrew was also on his fifth ale and the evening was still young.

Bruce placed his arm around Andrew's shoulder and said softly, 'Look, Andrew, we all have our prejudices, our likes and dislikes. The colour black is one of my dislikes. Is anything wrong with that?' Again, a sympathetic murmur rose from the group.

'No, Bruce,' Andrew replied in like manner. 'But why go to live among a people with a colour you dislike? This bothers me Bruce, and it should give you cause for concern.' Andrew was genuinely worried, and some guests were anxiously looking to Bruce for some positive response.

Bruce was quick to sense the mood of his friends as eager faces turned in his direction. 'Very well, Andrew.' Bruce became serious. 'Tell me what you would do if you inherited a flourishing, four-hundred acre estate, groomed and developed by the toil and sweat of your father and uncle? What if your inheritance depended on your continuing to run the estate or lose it?' Bruce revealed the condition his uncle set.

A moment of awkward quietness overshadowed the party. It was as if their host, Bruce, was held against the wall of his own living room and forced to reveal private details of his family. Andrew looked at Bruce with surprise. His heavily furrowed brow told an unspoken tale of toil and of worry. He broke the silence by repeating the revelation. 'You mean, you would lose your inheritance if you don't go?'

'Yes, Andrew. That's the long and short of it. That's why I'm going.'

'Oh, well, I'm sorry, Bruce. I should not have insisted, nor should you have told us.' Andrew lowered his head apologetically.

'Never mind, ol' boy.' Bruce tried to brush aside the embarrassment. 'Come on, it's a party. Let's drink!' He looked at his empty mug, then headed toward the bar.

'Hi, Bruce, darling.' He was greeted by Simone at the bar. 'I'm going to miss you.' Simone's face was flushed from gin and tonic.

'I'll miss you, too, Simone,' Bruce empathised, embracing her shoulders.

Sandra took her father's mug for refilling. She smiled at Simone's drunken behaviour, then exploded in laughter at what Simone said to her father in a faked foreign accent. 'But you'll soon forget me when you're in the arms of one of those romantic and sexy black beauties, dancing the . . .'

'Shut up, Simone!' Bruce reacted angrily, drawing away from her. His stomach knotted in revulsion at the idea of physically embracing a black woman.

Simone was jolted by Bruce's sudden outburst. 'What did I say?' Her inebriation was heightened by confusion so that her eyes became tear-filled. 'I was only having fun, Bruce.' She pleaded for forgiveness. 'I'm sorry, darling.'

'Okay, okay, forget it!' Bruce felt embarrassed. 'I'm sorry, too,' he apologised. 'I didn't mean to be rough with you.' He took the mug of ale from his daughter, noticing the shock in her eyes. He winked and smiled to her, then turned to rejoin the group, leaving Simone at the bar.

'What did I say to upset your father?' Simone asked Sandra with glazed eyes. 'It was only a joke.' Simone was still distressed. 'And now, I've spoilt the party. I always spoil parties.' She could no longer restrain the tears which flooded her cheeks.

'Come on now, Simone,' Sandra took her hand. 'Maybe you

ought to sit for a while.' She led her to the old chesterfield in the kitchen-diner. Simone sat heavily, then reclined. Sandra placed a cushion under her head and raised her feet.

'How is she?' asked Linda, a neighbour and school friend of Sandra who was helping at the bar.

'She's okay, I think. She had too much to drink, that's all.' Sandra was more concerned, however, with her father's sudden and unusual reaction to a seemingly harmless and jocular remark.

'You know San, I hear these black girls are really like that,' Linda whispered.

'Like what?'

'You know, romantic and sexy. More so than us.' Linda giggled embarrassingly.

'That's only a myth.' Sandra dismissed the belief that sexual prowess is superior in blacks.

'How do you know it's not true?' Linda persisted.

'How do you know it *is* true?' Sandra posed the rhetorical question which left Linda shrugging a wordless response.

CHAPTER THREE

'GOOD TO see you back, Henry.' Dr Korbinsky was bent over Henry Knowles probing his chest with a stethoscope. 'You left us for quite some time, much more than I anticipated.' He hung the stethoscope around his neck while checking Henry's pulse.

Henry shifted his gaze in the direction of Clifford Johnson. Then, with some effort, raised his left hand feebly in greeting.

Clifford answered cheerfully, 'Hello, Henry.'

'Oh, yes,' Dr Korbinsky remembered, 'Clifford has been waiting for you.'

Clifford approached Henry in his usual boisterous manner, unmindful of the atmosphere of gloom about the room. He sat gently beside Henry, clasped his left hand in both of his, then shook his head saying, 'You devil! You gave us quite a scare. So, I'm warning you, Henry, you better be around when Bruce arrives on Friday!'

The beaming smile which finally formed on Henry's face electrified the room. Clifford could not contain his joy and laughed for Henry.

Dr Korbinsky, too, joined in the joy of the moment. 'That's the spirit, Henry,' Dr Korbinsky knew the therapeutic value of laughter. 'That's the spirit,' he repeated.

But while Dr Korbinsky and Clifford may have paid little heed to the teardrops which rolled down Henry's withered cheeks, not so nurse Beatrice Andrews. She was fishing in her handbag for a kerchief to wipe her own tears of joy.

'That's very good news Henry,' Clifford said finally. 'It is wonderful that Bruce has agreed to take up the challenge to keep the tradition.'

The smile on Henry's lips had faded now. His countenance was now one of tranquillity and contentment. His eyes were closed, his breathing free and easy.

'I think he is asleep now, Cliff,' Dr Korbinsky whispered. 'The good news has done him well.'

'Yes, doc,' Clifford replied in a subdued voice, but lacking conviction. 'It certainly has,' he repeated, gently replacing Henry's hand at his side.

Dr Korbinsky glanced at Clifford, for he did not fail to notice the sudden change in Clifford's mood of optimism to one of concern and doubt.

'Well, nurse,' Dr Korbinsky addressed nurse Beatrice Andrews, 'you should take your rest now. I will ask Mable to keep an eye on Mr Knowles and to wake you in case of emergency.'

'All right, doctor. Thank you.' Beatrice Andrews was professional. She proceeded to pull the covers over Henry's feet when the doctor and Clifford left the room.

'Cliff, what's bothering you?' Dr Korbinsky was direct. 'Don't you share Henry's pleasure at his nephew's return?'

Clifford smiled, then shook his head in amazement. 'You are very perceptive, doc.'

'That's the nature of my occupation.' He did not return Clifford's smile. 'Want to talk about it over a drink at Henry's expense?' He smiled at his suggestion.

'Why not,' Clifford answered in a more relaxed tone. 'Henry would approve, I'm sure.' They sat at the living room bar off the kitchen.

'Mable,' Clifford called.

'Yes, Mr Clifford.' Mable entered from the kitchen, wiping her hands anxiously on her apron.

'Do you have any of your famous rum punch?' It was a favourite concoction of everyone who tried it.

'Yes, sir, Mr Clifford. I always keep a bottle handy.'

'Good. Let's have two tall ones for doctor and I.'

'Yes, sir, Mr Clifford.'

'So, what's the problem?' Dr Korbinsky prompted Clifford.

'It's a long story which began way back when Bruce was just about twelve years of age.' Clifford related the entire series of events involving Bruce's unhappy experience of his mother's death, his father's affair with the former housekeeper Margaret, his hatred for black people, his refusal to write his father from England and his refusal to attend his father's funeral three years ago.

Dr Korbinsky sat in silence as Clifford unfolded the story without pause. He sipped his rum punch occasionally, stirred the crushed ice in clockwise fashion with the straw and did not realise Clifford had come to the end of the story.

'That's the problem,' Clifford said, turning to Dr Korbinsky. Both remained silent as the full significance of the revelations began to emerge. Clifford refilled his glass, saying, 'The question is, why has Bruce decided to return to a home of bitter memories?'

'Beats me,' Dr Korbinsky answered as he analysed the situation. 'But my guess is, time may have healed his wounds.'

'Spoken like a true doctor,' Clifford joked. 'But if so, why did he refuse to attend his father's funeral?'

'Because the object of his resentment was still physically present,' the doctor suggested. 'But now, it is no more, hence likewise his resentment.'

'Assuming that to be the case, doc, then what of his hatred for black people? Would he be healed of this as well?'

Their conversation developed into an academic discussion on the psychology of attitudes and human behaviour. Bruce Knowles and his motives for returning were being critically examined by two of the closest friends of the Knowles family. They agreed, finally, that after twenty-five years in England, Bruce should be a changed man. Therefore, it was presumptuous to form opinions concerning his motives for returning to Knowles Gardens and Riversdale Plantations.

Dr Korbinsky glanced at his wristwatch. 'Should be on my way to the hospital, Cliff.' He drank the remaining punch in his glass. 'I must say, this has been a very stimulating exercise.' Then, he called Mable to ask her to look in on Henry while the nurse was

[21]

resting. 'Potent stuff, that punch of yours, but, mighty good.' They all laughed.

'It was nice talking to you, doc. You have helped me to keep an open mind about Bruce.' Clifford was truly thankful. 'When you have become so close to a family, you want to protect their interest as if it were your own.'

'I understand you, Cliff. Family doctors feel the same way,' Dr Korbinsky assured him. 'But don't ever forget, Bruce is also family.' Having said this, Dr Korbinsky dismounted his stool, picked up his briefcase and left.

Clifford turned to Mable. 'Did Eugene tell you about our meeting tomorrow?'

'Yes, Mr Clifford. He tell me you have very important news for us.' Her face lit up.

'I certainly do!' Clifford emphasised. He smiled, then laughed, shaking his head from side to side. Still grinning, he said, 'You should have seen the smile on Mr Knowles's face when he heard the news!'

'I so happy, too, Mr Clifford, I cannot wait to see my Brucie.' Mable's eyes revealed her longing. Then, suddenly, she froze, placed both hands over her mouth realising she had betrayed Eugene's trust. 'Oh, my God!' She exclaimed, turning to leave.

'Mable,' Clifford stopped her. She turned slowly and looked at him with such guilt that he smiled and asked, 'Have you been listening to our conversation?'

'Oh, no! Mr Clifford, sir,' Mable defended her honour, 'I would never do dat! Oh, no!' Mable crossed her forehead, lips and heart to denote truth. 'Cross my heart!' she said finally, with utter conviction.

'Then, Eugene told you.'

Mable dropped her head in surrender, then nodded slowly, feeling as defenceless as a child caught with hand in the cookie jar.

Clifford smiled at the gesture of innocence, then laughed. They both laughed happily.

'Someone said that parting is sweet sorrow. I can understand why.' Betty was reclined in bed, caressing a hot cup of tea.

'I know what you mean,' Bruce said thoughtfully. 'It is really sad to leave your friends, the people you love, trust, and understand.'

Betty agreed. 'It reminds me of when I had to leave my friends and foster parents in Leamington to come to London.'

'But life went on. We managed to build for ourselves a stable foundation, good jobs, nice home, and a new group of reliable friends,' Bruce added.

'And a wonderful daughter,' Betty smiled.

'Yes,' Bruce agreed. 'She is certainly excited about this move.'

'I suppose everything is happening for her all at once. Her first airplane ride, the first time to a tropical island, first time to meet one of your relatives.' Betty paused, then said regretfully, 'As a matter of fact, it is the first time, too, I'll be meeting one of my in-laws.'

'Look, Betty, you know why I never wanted to go back.' Bruce became defensive.

'I understand, Bruce. I am not blaming you for that. I would probably have felt the same way if that had happened to me.'

'Do you really mean that?' Bruce looked surprised.

'Yes, love.' Betty held his hand.

'Well, what made you change your mind? You always thought I over-reacted to what was a perfectly natural thing.'

'Yes, I did,' Betty admitted, 'but, that was before we had San.'

'What do you mean?'

Betty cleared her throat. 'I've wanted to say this to you for a long time, but the subject never came up till now.' Betty was soft-spoken as with all true confessions. 'Before we had San, I had no idea what a mother's love for her child was really like. As I told you before, I lost my mother when I was three and I was brought up at Mason Lodge Orphanage. I never had the real experience of mother's love, you see?'

'Hmm.' Bruce understood.

'So, as San grew up, I often wondered what would I do if I lost her. This sounds silly, now that she is so grown, but it frightened me at the time. You remember when I used to be so over-protective? That's what you used to say, Bruce, and you were right.' Betty drank a mouthful of tea. 'Well, it turned out this mother-and-child love works both ways. San became so depend-ent on me during her tender years that she hated it when I started work, when I went to the ladies social club, even when I showed affection towards friends.'

'She felt threatened, that's all,' Bruce concluded.

'And so were you, Bruce, when you saw Margaret taking your mother's place.' Betty smiled at her husband.

'Not threatened, Betty, mad!' Bruce recalled. 'So mad, I could have killed them both for doing that to my mother!'

'So, I was wrong.' Betty squeezed her husband's hand. 'I would have felt the same way.'

'Thank you for saying so. You have no idea how it makes me feel.'

'I do.' Betty nodded with understanding. 'And, by agreeing to go back, you are taking a big step toward forgiveness, and I know how that makes me feel to be Mrs Bruce Knowles.'

He would have shown Betty how much he appreciated her kind and loving words with much more than a kiss, but the telephone had a disturbing ring about it.

'Hello.' Bruce answered. 'Yes, this is Bruce Knowles.' He sat up, alert to the party at the other end. 'Yes ... At what time, did you say? ... Twelve o'clock? ... Yes ... All right, thank you.' Bruce replaced the receiver, then looked at his watch.

'What was that about?' Betty asked anxiously.

'We are on the midday flight instead of this evening. From midnight there will be a national strike on the island, so we have to arrive before it.'

'That means we have only three hours to complete our packing and get to the airport.' Betty jumped out of bed and into Sandra's room to wake her. When she came back Bruce was already telephoning Clifford Johnson on the island.

CHAPTER FOUR

SAMUEL HARRIS was unhappy because he had not completed balancing his accounts for the day, yet was summoned to Knowles Gardens 'Well, Eugene, aren't you going to let me know what this is all about? And where is Mr Johnson? Does he think everyone has to wait on him?'

'Why are you so impatient, Sam?' Eugene wore a teasing smile, which infuriated Samuel the more.

'I suppose this is a big joke for you, eh?' Samuel pushed back his spectacles which continually slid down his flat nose. 'I have deadlines, you don't.'

'Mr Johnson looks after the legal affairs of Riversdale Plantations, and he has asked us here to discuss the future of Riversdale. That's all I know.'

'What future?' Samuel exclaimed. 'You know as well as I do that Riversdale is going to become another agricultural station. And you know what that means.'

'Only a change of management,' Eugene provoked, smiling.

'You mean from management to mismanagement.'

'Well, thank you very much for your vote of confidence, Sam,' Eugene smiled.

'Don't forget I count the monies, so I know what I am talking about.' Samuel was now relaxed. 'It is really a shame to transfer this thriving estate to the Agricultural Department.'

'Maybe they won't,' Eugene smiled.

'There you go again.' Samuel could not understand Eugene's apparent indifference in the face of the impending death of Henry Knowles, and the imminent collapse of Riversdale

Plantations. 'You are really taking this lightly, as if you couldn't care less what becomes of Riversdale.' He pushed back his spectacles once more.

'I have always been an optimist, Sam, even when the odds were heavily against me. Riversdale will be all right.'

Samuel and Eugene looked down the corridor when Clifford and Mable stepped down from the living room. Clifford stopped at the door to Henry's bedroom to inquire about him. Mable continued to the office.

'Hello, Mr Samuel,' she greeted with a warm smile. 'I don' see you dese days.'

'Hello, Mable, how are you?' Samuel responded in kind. 'I am too busy in town, handling everything by myself. But I'll try to visit more often.'

'I always see Eugie, doh.' Mable caressed Eugene's shoulder in greeting.

'Mabes, I'm not single like Sam. When I leave work I have a wife to go home to. And, when I'm not at home, well, where else could I be but with you, my second mamma? But Sam,' Eugene laughed in anticipation of his quip, 'he is still running around chasing the ladies. He has no time for you.'

They all laughed heartily, but Samuel felt he should set the record straight. 'Believe me, Mable, Eugene is spreading false rumours.' He glanced at Eugene, and pointed a warning finger, then fidgeted with his spectacles.

'Anyway, what you all want?' Mable changed the subject. 'Tea, coffee, punch, or what?'

'I could take a beer,' Samuel answered.

'Me, too,' Eugene ordered.

'Okay.' Mable left, passing Clifford in the corridor. 'I goin' for drinks, Mr Clifford. What you want?'

'Punch, of course, what else?'

Mable laughed appreciatively and hurried along, while Clifford stepped into the office. He greeted Samuel and Eugene, sat down heavily. 'Well, Henry is definitely on his last lap. Nurse Andrews believes that he gave up the fight from the time he knew that Bruce was coming back.' He paused briefly to shake his head, then continued, 'Well, let's get down to planning Bruce's welcome.'

Samuel looked at Eugene, confusedly. Eugene could not resist the smile which formed on his face as he watched Sam's anxiety mount in his eyes above his slipping spectacles. Sam was not amused and quickly turned to Clifford for clarification. 'Excuse me, Mr Johnson. Do I know this person, Bruce?'

'Oh! I'm sorry, Samuel,' Clifford apologised. 'I should have told you before. Bruce Knowles is the son of Charles Knowles. He has been living in England for the past twenty-five years. He inherits the estate and is coming over tomorrow to assume control.'

'Now, that is good news,' exclaimed Samuel, repositioning his spectacles.

'Well, I don't know,' Clifford remarked softly.

'As far as I am concerned, Mr Johnson, the estate would do better privately than in the hands of the Agricultural Department.' Samuel was emphatic.

'You are probably right on that score,' Clifford conceded. 'But, whether private or public, we still depend on men to manage.' He paused when Mable brought in the refreshments, then continued, 'We will discuss your part first, Mable.' He took a long sip of punch while Mable sat next to Eugene. Then, he exhaled a sigh of relief as the cool, citric mixture drenched his parched throat. 'This must be the best drink in the world, Mable.'

'Better dan beer?' Mable asked, eyeing both Eugene and Samuel.

'Oh, yes, by far,' Clifford complimented.

'Thank you, Mr Clifford.' Mable folded her arms in satisfaction.

'Okay,' Clifford commenced, 'Bruce is married with a daughter of eighteen. That means you will have to move up to servant's quarters, Mable.'

'Yes, Mr Clifford,' Mable replied.

'But I guess, when Henry goes, you could move back downstairs.'

'Oh, no, Mr Clifford,' Mable replied shyly, 'only if Mr Bruce want me to.'

'Fair enough. The gardeners will help you move the furniture as before.'

The telephone rang. Eugene, sitting nearest to it, answered. 'Hello, Knowles Gardens ... Yes, he's here ... Okay, hold on.' He passed the receiver to Clifford.

'Clifford Johnson speaking ... Yes ... From Bruce Knowles? Okay, go ahead...' A long pause followed while Clifford listened and scribbled notes on the pad before him. 'Okay, thank you.' He replaced the receiver. 'That was Cable and Wireless. The Knowles are arriving this evening instead. The airlines brought the flight forward to beat the strike.'

'But the strike was called off this morning,' Eugene commented.

'I guess their plans were made ahead of time,' Clifford figured. 'However, let's continue with our plans. Mable, you may as well call in the gardeners and make your move right away.'

'Yes, Mr Clifford.' Mable left.

'Which one of you would like to go for the family at the airport, or should we send a taxi? Clifford glanced at the two men.

'Would be better if one of us met them,' Eugene suggested. 'We would not be entirely strangers, so to speak.'

'I have to return to work,' Samuel explained. 'My books must be completed today.'

'I'll go,' Eugene volunteered without much enthusiasm.

'Take the station wagon. You'll need plenty room for luggage.' Clifford paused thoughtfully, then concluded, 'Well, that's it for now. Other matters can be dealt with when Bruce is here.'

Samuel rose from his chair, turned to Clifford and said, 'Would you believe I never knew Charles had a son? After all these years, it takes the death of his uncle to bring him to life.' He shook his head and smiled.

'There is a lot you don't know, Samuel,' Clifford shook his head likewise. 'But, sooner or later, you'll find out and the mystery will be solved.'

*　　*　　*

[28]

Bruce sat between Betty and Sandra in the departure lounge at London Airport. The rush was over. It was time for his pipe. He reached for his tobacco pouch in the inner pocket of his tweed jacket. 'Damn!' He interjected. 'I forgot my tobacco.' He searched his other pockets nervously. 'Better get some more while I'm still in civilised country.' He stood and headed for the kiosk.

'Are the people really uncivilised on the island, mom?' Sandra asked her mother in disbelief.

'No, dear,' Betty replied reassuringly. 'They are West Indians, just like the ones who attend your school. Your father speaks like that whenever he is upset.'

'I hope he doesn't speak that way among the people on the island. They would certainly become very angry.' Sandra was concerned.

'I don't think he would, dear. But, when he is angry he can say anything.'

'I know,' Sandra laughed. 'He told Simone to shut up at our party because she got him angry.' Sandra continued to laugh. 'Simone was a bit drunk, of course, but, dad didn't like what she said.'

'And, what was that, dear?' Betty had not been aware of the incident.

'Something to do with how he was going to forget her when the black beauties on the island get him.' Sandra laughed aloud. 'I thought that was funny, and so did Simone, but, dad got really upset, you know, and I wondered why.'

'Well, that is your father, all right.'

'Does he hate black people, mom?' Sandra's question was direct and unexpected.

'Why do you ask that?' Betty hedged, since she had no immediate reply that would satisfy the curiosity of Sandra's open mind and, at the same time, protect her from the knowledge of her father's bigotry.

'Well, dad wasn't keen on going back. He never returned once after all these years. He told me he didn't like the island. Simone's mention of black beauties upsetting him, you know, and things like that.' Sandra shrugged her shoulders as she tried to fit the pieces together. 'And now, he refers to them as uncivilised, the same way the National Front refers to black people here, in England.'

'Well, what can I say to you?' Betty was surprised at her daughter's reasoning. 'I suppose, whether he knew it or not, your father was saying something to you from his behaviour.' Betty paused, then turned to face Sandra. 'San,' she took her daughter by the hand and continued almost in a whisper. 'Keep this a secret between us.' Sandra nodded agreement. 'Your father is not fond of black people. One day, I will explain to you why. But, for now, it is good for you to know this about him. Believe me, San, he has good reason to feel this way, but after all these years, one would think he would have outgrown it.' Betty squeezed her daughter's hand as if to ask whether she understood.

'Outgrown what, mom?' Sandra's eager eyes revealed her burning curiosity.

'Oh, San, it's a long story. I'll tell you all about it one day soon. But, just remember what I've told you for now.' She looked away from Sandra to see Bruce returning. 'Here comes dad.'

Bruce was already smoking his pipe. Before sitting, he offered to get them refreshment. Betty suggested they waited to enjoy what the airline was offering. Bruce sat heavily, no longer agitated, but calmed by the narcotic in the tobacco. 'Any minute now,' he said.

Just then, the speakers called passengers for their flight to report to the embarking point.

'That's us.' Bruce stood up. 'Well, this is it, San, your first trip overseas.' Bruce caressed his daughter about her shoulders. 'It's going to be fun.'

Sandra felt a lump in her throat. 'I am so excited,' she stammered, 'I'm almost scared.' She curled her arm around her father's waist as they joined the queue.

Betty smiled proudly.

Eugene looked at his wristwatch. It was ten after five. The

evening was warm and Monique was in no hurry. She eased her moist body closer to his and moaned softly.

'Time for me to go, Nicky,' Eugene yawned. 'I have a long, rough drive ahead of me tonight.' He kissed her lips, then pulled himself away, reluctantly, to lie on his back.

'You've got plenty time still.' Monique rolled her body over him, kissed his closed eyes, then his nose and finally his lips.

Eugene responded affectionately, squeezing her body ever closer to his. 'I'm going to hurry back, so I hope you'll stay awake.' He sighed as he reclaimed his lips.

'Take it easy on the road, though?' Monique and Eugene had been married for four years. She was his only love, as far as she knew, and considered herself very fortunate in a culture which pays lip service to family, Christianity and morality, yet practises sexual promiscuity. She kissed him once more. 'I love you, Eugie,' she cried, looking him straight in the eye from her vantage point. 'Remember, I am a jealous woman,' she added, smiling.

'I'll remember,' Eugene joked. 'I'll be discreet about it.'

'About what?' Monique egged on playfully.

'You know, with the girl I'm taking out tonight,' he teased, holding a rigid face which broke up into fits of laughter as he tried to ward off Monique's attack of fists upon his hairy chest. He finally held her in warm embrace.

'I would die if you ever did that to me, Eugie,' Monique cried tearfully.

'You know I never would.'

'I know,' Monique sobbed, burying her lips on his neck.

'Hey, what's this?' Eugene reacted when he felt her warm tears on his neck. 'What's the tears for?'

'Nothing,' Monique replied, 'I am just being silly.'

'C'mon Nicky, stop this nonsense,' Eugene coaxed, 'I was joking.'

'I was joking, too, but I can't bear even the thought of losing you.'

'Well, you don't have to,' Eugene reassured her as he rose to go to the bathroom.

Monique lay back in bed, peaceful and contented. As she

[31]

listened to the fall of the shower, her eyes closed slowly and soon, she was in deep slumber.

Eugene emerged, fully dressed. 'It's five thirty already. I'll see you later, Nicky.' He turned to see his wife asleep, just like a baby. He smiled, shook his head and whispered, 'You have no idea how much I love you, girl.' He bent to kiss her lips. 'Sweet dreams, my love.' Monique stirred when he drew the covers over her.

'We are now approaching Melville Hall Airport.' The pilot's voice was crisp. Sandra looked out of the window of the small aircraft and saw the outline of the rugged mountains against the evening sky. Then, the aeroplane began its descent.

Sandra held her breath in fear when the craft dropped suddenly into an air pocket. She was not alone, for the nun two seats ahead of her made the sign of the cross. The mountains disappeared as the aircraft emerged, it seemed just a few feet above a flat meadow. Suddenly, there was the runway, and the landing moments after.

Sandra could not take her eyes away from the window as the plane taxied to the reception. 'What are these strange, little, flashing lights darting about in the air, dad?'

'They are called fireflies. They are night insects with bellies that glow in the dark. The island is full of strange creatures.'

The aircraft stopped. Sandra's excitement began to mount even more.

There were only four white people in the group of arrivals, one of whom was the nun. Betty and Sandra were listening attentively to what Mother Rosa was saying.

'We live close to one of the most beautiful botanic gardens in the Caribbean and Knowles Gardens is also very beautiful. I've been there many times with students to see the exotic plants,' Mother Rosa complimented.

'I hope you will continue to visit us, Mother.' Betty extended an open invitation.

'Thank you, I will, especially to visit our new student, Sandra,' she assumed.

Sandra smiled shyly. It was her first encounter with a Catholic nun. She wondered what it would be like going to a Catholic school. Would she be accepted?

'All cleared now.' Bruce brought the last suitcase to the pile. 'I guess I'll have to get us a taxi.' He left the group and approached the exit door.

'Excuse me sir,' Eugene called. Bruce turned in his direction. 'Are you Mr Knowles?'

'Yes.' Bruce's eyes showed no curiosity, no warmth, at the sight of this black man hailing him.

'I'm Eugene St Rose, sir, overseer at Riversdale Plantations. Welcome to Dominica.' He extended a hand in greeting. 'I've come to take you and the family.'

Bruce Knowles did not shake Eugene's hand. 'Oh yes? Jolly good. Our luggage is over here.' Bruce pointed.

Eugene dropped his hand, smiled to conceal the rage which began to churn within him. 'Sure.' He followed Bruce to the women. 'Mrs Knowles, Miss Knowles, Mother.' Eugene greeted them with a smile, and they reciprocated.

'Would you have room for one more passenger?' Bruce asked.

'Yes, we do.' Eugene was cold.

'I hope I won't be inconveniencing you.' Mother Rosa sensed his tension.

'No, Mother, we have a station wagon. There is sufficient room,' Eugene smiled.

'God bless you, my son.'

'Thank you, Mother,' Eugene acknowledged, then opened the rear door of the wagon and began loading the luggage while his passengers were deciding where they would be seated.

'May I sit at the front, dad?'

'No, San, that's for the driver.'

He meant to say, 'Not beside the driver,' Eugene thought.

'But, there is an extra seat, dad,' Sandra insisted.

'Sandra, you heard your father.' Betty knew the reason for Bruce's denial.

'Okay.' Sandra was displeased, but smiled to Mother Rosa when she sat beside her.

[33]

'It's a long drive to the capital. You may rest your head on my shoulder if you feel sleepy, Sandra.' Mother Rosa placed a soft hand on Sandra's to comfort her.

Sandra smiled in response. 'I hope all the teachers at the school are as kind as you, Mother.'

'They are,' Mother Rosa assured her. 'They are also very strict about school work, though.'

The engine roared to a start and the journey began. Eugene remained silent throughout the drive, not because he was concentrating on avoiding the many potholes in the road, but because he was hurting inside. Bruce Knowles had insulted him at their first meeting, and he was not going to let Bruce forget it. 'Mabes was right,' Eugene was thinking. 'He hates the black man. So why the hell is he here?' Eugene slapped his hand on the steering wheel to vent his anger. 'Okay, comrade Bruce,' he mused, 'welcome to Dominica!'

Darkness fell rapidly as the road curled its way deep into the hinterland. The early moon had already joined the stars to pour forth an astral brilliance on the lush vegetation which flanked the roadside. Fireflies darted about in every direction painting luminous, abstract designs against the dark shadows beneath the trees. And the distant croaking of the mountain frogs punctuated the monotony of the shrilling crickets.

Suddenly, but steadily, Eugene brought the wagon to a stop. The silence was tense as the party watched the huge reptile glide across the narrow road. The boa was about eight inches across and about twelve feet long. Its sinuous body glistened in the beams of the headlights, displaying a beautiful array of colours.

Sandra loosened her grip on Mother Rosa's hand when the creature finally disappeared into the bushes. The nun crossed herself automatically, whispering thanks to God. Betty exhaled a heavy sigh of relief as the wagon continued on its way. Bruce cleared his throat, and would have welcomed his pipe, but alas! Eugene maintained silence.

The street lights of the village of Roger became visible as the descent from the mountain road began. In the distance the sparkle of the Caribbean Sea in the moonlight was beautiful to behold.

'How far again to go?' Bruce broke the silence.

'About five miles,' Eugene replied coldly.

'Well, look at these beautiful houses!' Betty exclaimed, much to her surprise. 'They should cost a pretty penny.'

'These are probably the aristocrats of the island,' Bruce remarked sardonically.

'Not really,' Mother Rosa corrected. 'People of all walks of life live here. Some of our lay teachers live here and they are people of modest means.'

'Well, I certainly would like to see where the aristocrats live,' Bruce became curious.

'At Knowles Gardens, for instance.' Mother Rosa touched Sandra on the hand. 'So you are an aristocrat, young lady.' Sandra laughed at what for her was a joke, but Mother Rosa continued. 'In fact, Knowles Gardens is perhaps the best example of what the aristocratic setting was like in the old colonial days.'

Eugene smiled at the way the nun put it. He sensed a lament in her clear, unadulterated Irish accent, a nostalgia for the return of the past. 'But, gone are the days of colonial domination,' Eugene was thinking. 'Riversdale Plantations is, indeed, the last vestige of the colonial, landed aristocracy and will be changed someday.'

The sea waves tumbled in thunder and foam upon the dark grey sands along the beach. The fresh smell of sand and salt was new to Sandra. She inhaled deeply as she watched the froth rush back again and again to be consumed by wave after wave.

Traffic was increasing. Eugene dimmed the beams for an approaching cyclist. In the distance, flickering lights outlined the curve of the Roseau harbour, just for an instant, as the wagon turned in the direction of the city. Sandra was excited. Bombarded by new smells, calypso music, a strange language, laughter and black faces, she found herself suddenly in a new world, a world she had to understand by living and participating in. Would it be difficult, or would she become like her father?

'What are the people like, Mother?' Sandra wanted some

immediate answers. She remembered her father had not answered her. So she turned to someone who knew.

'Very warm, very friendly, full of fun, very crazy sometimes,' Mother Rosa laughed. 'They are very religious, and that is what keeps them so happy in their poverty.'

Eugene clenched his teeth at this last remark. 'Religion is the opiate of the people. Was it Karl Marx who said that, or was it Lenin?' he thought. 'How right they must have been. Religion has kept the developing world in poverty, and it has been the greatest ally of capitalism.' Eugene's thought unfolded in silent response to Mother Rosa's theory of the co-existence of poverty and happiness in religion.

'They sound interesting,' Sandra observed, 'and they do carry happy smiling faces,' she continued, when she saw the group of four standing at the street corner talking.

Eugene lowered the gear shift as the wagon approached an incline. The engine groaned under the heavy load. He turned to the left at the top of the hill and headed for the convent.

'Well, Sandra, Mr and Mrs Knowles, I thank you very much for your kindness and pleasant company.' Mother Rosa expressed her appreciation.

'Don't mention it, Mother,' Bruce shook his head. 'We have been blessed by your presence and are fortunate to have met you, especially Sandra, who will be attending your school.'

The wagon came to a stop at the entrance of the convent. Eugene opened the door for the nun and retrieved her suitcase. By that time Mother Rosa had summoned the nightwatchman for assistance.

'Thank you again, son. God be with you,' Mother Rosa smiled to Eugene.

'Thank you, Mother,' Eugene replied, not knowing whether he should return her good wishes.

Knowles Gardens was only half a mile away along the river valley.

'This is the Botanic Gardens that Mother Rosa talked about,' Betty pointed for Sandra. 'Isn't it beautiful, even at night?'

Suddenly, the road surface changed from oil to dirt, causing a cloud of white dust behind the wagon. Not far off in the distance, Eugene could see Mable standing at the outer door of the kitchen like the biblical good servant who stayed awake awaiting the return of the master.

CHAPTER FIVE

SANDRA AND her mother were exhausted from the long, rough journey from the airport. They sat on the settee while Bruce watched Eugene unload the wagon. Mable was the object of Sandra's intense gaze. She had noticed the warm smile and sparkling eyes when Mable greeted her father.

'Welcome home, Brucie,' Mable had approached with open arms just like a mother would to her loved one.

Bruce had replied, 'Hello, and who are you?' He kept his distance, raised no hands and exchanged no smile.

Mable's hands dropped slowly as the intoxicating joy of her memory was dampened by the frigid forgetfulness of Bruce Knowles. 'I . . .' she began her introduction, but her voice failed her.

'You must be one of the servants?' Bruce offered a reply.

Mable nodded. But Betty could not help noticing the gloom into which Mable sank. 'Hello,' she intervened and extended her hand.

'Mrs Bruce, welcome home.' Without hesitation, Mable took Betty's hand in greeting.

'Hello, I'm Sandra. What's your name?' Sandra followed her mother.

'Hello, Miss Sandra,' Mable beamed. 'I am Mable, de housekeeper. Please to meet you.'

Mable had offered to prepare supper, but Betty said they would settle for a light snack of chocolate and toast.

'There is no hurry, Mable,' Betty had said, 'we will wait until we are settled in our rooms.'

Sandra continued to gaze at Mable. She observed how strangely Mable looked at her father. There was a look of saddened joy in her eyes, an expression of pride in her faint smile and her body still poised to receive that embrace which her father denied.

Sandra recalled the talk with her mother at London Airport. That her father was not fond of black people seemed obvious. Why else didn't he shake Mable's hand? Sandra was becoming concerned. Was she seeing a side of her father she had not seen before? Was he racially prejudiced?

'Well, er, what's your name again?' Bruce addressed Eugene when the unloading was completed.

'Eugene.'

'I guess I'll be seeing you, when, on Monday?' Bruce inquired.

'I believe Mr Johnson will be seeing you tomorrow. Following that he will advise us on your wishes.'

'Good show, then, and thank you for your assistance.'

'Goodnight, all.' Eugene waved and smiled to Mable who saw him to the door.

'Goodnight, Eugie.' Mable closed the door and proceeded to show the Knowles their rooms. Then she turned to Betty and said, 'I in de kitchen, mam, if you want me.'

'All right, Mable,' Betty replied. 'Forget the toast and just make us the hot chocolate, please.'

'Yes, mam.'

The telephone rang. Mable answered it at the bar. Clifford Johnson wanted Bruce Knowles. 'Hol' on Mr Clifford, I callin' him for you.' Mable placed the receiver on the counter and walked down the corridor to Bruce's room. She knocked on the door and shouted, 'Mr Bruce, telephone for you.'

'Who is it?' Bruce called out.

'Mr Clifford, de lawyer, Mr Bruce.'

'All right, I'm coming.'

'Yes, Mr Bruce.' Mable smiled at Sandra when she walked passed her open door.

'Is that a swimming pool out there?' Sandra asked excitedly.

'Yes, Miss Sandra.'

'That's great!'

Bruce met Mable in the corridor. 'Where's the telephone, Mable?'

'On de counter, Mr Bruce.' Mable was following Bruce to show him its location, when Betty called out.

'Is the chocolate ready yet?'

'It still boilin', mam,' Mable called back.

'Boiling!' Betty repeated with astonishment. 'You don't boil chocolate. You'll ruin it.'

'You have to boil de cocoa first, mam. I not makin' it wif cocoa powder. I usin' de good cocoa wif spice, mam. It much better.' Mable smiled proudly.

Betty looked at Mable, somewhat confused. 'Oh, I see. I'm sorry.' She apologised before closing the bedroom door.

'It sounds nice,' Sandra commented.

'Wait till you tas'e it wif coconut milk,' Mable chuckled.

'Mable,' Sandra dropped her voice. 'Did you know my father before?'

'Oh, yes, Miss Sandra.' Mable's face lit up. 'Oh, yes. I raise him jus' like I was his mamma. When his mamma die...' Mable began, but stopped abruptly, as if the memory was best left alone.

'What happened when his mother died?' Sandra's curiosity was aroused, her tiredness vanished.

'I tell you nex' time, okay, Miss Sandra. I goin' an' finish de cocoa.' Mable left hurriedly before Sandra could continue her probing.

'You mean Henry is here in this house?' Bruce was saying on the telephone. 'Nurse who? ... Yes ... Well, I'll take a peep, naturally, but, I won't disturb them ... All right, Clifford ... Yes, see you in the morning.' Bruce replaced the receiver and looked at Mable in the kitchen. 'Mable,' he called.

'Yes, Mr Bruce.' She hurried to the bar.

'Would you show me Henry's room?'

'Yes, Mr Bruce.' Mable led him down the second corridor and pointed at the door without a word.

'Thank you,' whispered Bruce. He pushed it open gently. The

room had a typical hospital smell about it. He could not see Henry's face in the dim light, but nurse Beatrice, on the couch, was wide awake.

'Is that you, Mable?' Nurse Beatrice called softly.

'No,' replied Bruce, 'I am Bruce Knowles, Henry's nephew.'

Nurse Beatrice sprang to her feet, and approached the door. 'Good evening, sir. Your uncle is asleep at the moment.'

'How is he?' Bruce stepped aside to let the nurse onto the corridor to avoid disturbing Henry.

'Very critical, weak, being fed intravenously, but, reasonably alert when he's awake.'

'Is he in pain?'

'Occasionally, but he has medication for that.'

'What is wrong with him? I mean, eh, what is his sickness?' Bruce fumbled for words.

'Cancer, sir,' Nurse Beatrice replied without emotion. 'Terminal. According to Dr Korbinsky, your uncle has passed the expected time of survival for his condition. But the doctor will be in tomorrow, sir.'

'Well, thank you, very much, nurse. I'll see my uncle tomorrow.'

'You are welcome, sir, goodnight.' She closed the door gently behind her.

Mable met Bruce as she was leaving his room with the empty tray. 'Your cocoa inside, Mr Bruce. Goodnight an' sleep well.'

'Goodnight, Mable,' Bruce replied. 'Do have a good night's sleep.' Bruce, however, stopped briefly at the door.

When Mable stepped into the living room she looked back to catch Bruce gazing at her. In that brief moment, her heart leapt beneath her breasts. Bruce smiled to cover his embarrassment, and Mable returned his smile.

'Your chocolate is getting cold, love.' Betty was reclined in bed against the headboard sipping cocoa. She could not help noticing the smile her husband was carrying. 'Penny for your thoughts?' She inquired.

Bruce laughed. 'You know, it's strange the way Mable looks at me,' he said. 'There is something about her that is familiar.'

Bruce became thoughtful, then shrugged his shoulders to dismiss the possibility.

'I noticed that, too,' Betty agreed. 'She was so happy to see you, as if she expected you to embrace her. She was very disappointed when you didn't.'

'But why should she expect such greeting from a stranger?' Bruce sipped his cocoa.

'My feeling is you are not a stranger to her. She might have known you as a boy, and was obviously pleased to see you again after all these years.'

'Even if she did know me as a boy, I'm sure she would not expect warm greetings from me.' Bruce's voice hardened as sad memories of his childhood flashed in his mind. 'No one here should expect any kindness from me,' he added as an after-thought.

The silence which followed this declaration was disturbed only by the rushing flow of the Woodbridge River a few hundred yards away. Betty finished her drink, placed the cup on the bedside table and eased herself gently beneath the sheets.

'Ohhh! I'm so tired,' she yawned.

'However, it's strange what happened a while ago.' Bruce's thoughts were still occupied with Mable.

'Hm?' Betty was not attentive.

'You wanted to know why I was smiling?' Bruce asked.

'Uhum,' muttered a drowsy Betty.

'Well, as I passed Mable on the corridor just now she wished me a good night's sleep and I wished her the same. But, in that brief exchange, I felt a strange warmth come over me.' Bruce paused to recapture the feeling. 'I found myself smiling to her and she to me.'

'That's good,' Betty mumbled, as she turned herself in a more comfortable position, pulling the sheets over her head at the same time.

Bruce glanced at his wife, shook his head, smiled, then turned to kiss her. 'Goodnight love, sweet dreams.'

The flapping of wings and the crowing of roosters were unfamiliar sounds to Sandra. She yawned lazily, stretched her arms, then opened her eyes slowly to the blinding sunshine which flooded her room. Her watch registered ten minutes to seven. She jumped out of bed and hurried into the corridor overlooking the swimming pool to catch a glimpse of two red-breasted robins chirping melodiously, perched on a stalk of the pawpaw tree near the pool. They gazed at Sandra curiously, whistled softly as if to greet her, then flew towards the river.

Mable descended the steps from her upstairs quarters and saw Sandra admiring the exotic back garden. 'Good mornin', Miss Sandra,' she beamed.

'Good morning, Mable,' Sandra smiled at the stout, but affable, black woman who seemed to radiate warmth with every inch of her broad smile and glistening, white teeth.

'You sleep well?' Mable asked.

'Very well, thank you. I feel great. The air is so fresh and clean.' Sandra inhaled deeply.

'Dat's good, Miss Sandra. I hope your mamma an' papa will like it, too.' Mable's smile melted.

Sandra sensed a deep longing in Mable's voice, a kind of need to fill an emptiness in her being. 'I'm sure they will, Mable.'

Mable looked at Sandra admiringly. 'You lookin' so much like your gran'ma, pretty, an' kin', an' always smilin'.'

'Did you know daddy's mother?' Sandra became excited.

'Oh, yes,' Mable replied with obvious delight. 'She was de nices' person in de whole of Dominica. Everybody like her an' she treat everybody right.' But suddenly, Mable's countenance changed to one of remorse. 'I will never forget de day she die. Everybody cry for Miss Bella excep' dat ... dat ... Margaret.' Mable's eyes filled with tears, but the thought of Margaret caused her face to twist in hatred. 'Anyway, dat's a long time ago.' Mable shook off the sad memories, smiled at Sandra and proceeded to the kitchen.

Sandra stood with arms folded watching Mable wobble her fat buttocks towards the kitchen. She would have smiled at the spectacle, but instead she wondered at Mable's sudden mood swings, from joy to sadness to hatred and back to joy. 'And, who was Margaret, anyway?' Sandra murmured to herself.

Bruce sat up in bed, swung his legs to the floor and gazed fixedly at the mirror, deep in thought. Suddenly, he turned to Betty. His eyes narrowed and mouth opened to form a smile. 'It's Mable,' he muttered to himself. 'It has to be Mabes!' He shouted and began to laugh. 'Betty, Betty,' he shook her gently. 'Wake up, I've got news for you! Do you know who Mable is?'

'Hm?' Betty groaned and turned towards her husband. 'Only that she is our housekeeper.'

'Yes, and after all these years she is still here. Why didn't I recognise her?' Bruce felt ashamed.

Betty sat up fully awake now. 'Don't tell me she is the one who cared for you after your mother died?'

'I'm sure of it,' Bruce said softly. 'I saw it in her eyes last night.' Then, in a fit of anger, he cried, 'Why didn't she tell me?'

'I knew from the moment she greeted you there was some connection between you two. She was so excited to see you, Bruce. But how could you have known after all these years?' Betty felt the pain her husband must be feeling, and empathised.

'I wonder what she must think of me? How could I have done this to her?' Bruce was upset with himself now. 'I better renew my acquaintance immediately.' Bruce wasted no time, slipped on his robe and hurried to the kitchen. Betty followed at his heels.

Mable was setting the table for breakfast in the dining room. 'Good mornin', Mr Bruce.' Her smile was radiant.

'Good morning Mabes.' Bruce greeted her in the familiar way. 'And how are you today?'

'Fine, Mr Br...' Mable's voice choked. Her heart skipped a beat. She turned to see the provocative grin on Bruce's face as he looked at her.

He shook his head in wonder, his eyes filling with tears of joy. 'Come here, Mabes.' Bruce stretched out his arms to her.

Her reaction was instantaneous. 'Oh, Brucie, you rem'ber me?' She cried as her tears rolled down her cheeks, easily.

'I'm sorry, Mabes,' Bruce apologised. 'I should have recognised you sooner. I'm really sorry. Will you forgive me?'

Betty and Sandra stood in the hallway watching the scene, their eyes flooded with tears, grinning from ear to ear.

'Come, Mabes,' Bruce took her by the hand, 'let me tell my family who you really are.'

'I know all about you, Mable,' Betty started. 'Bruce said you were like a mother to him when his own mother died, and we want to thank you very much for that.'

'You don' have to fank me for dat, mam,' Mable tried to shy away from praise. 'I love Brucie like he is my own chil'. Somebody have to take care of Brucie, an' I fank God he choose me.'

'And I thank God, too, you were there, Mabes, when I needed someone.' He hugged her once more. 'I am glad you are here instead of Margaret,' he added.

'Margaret!' Mable exclaimed, drawing away from Bruce as if he had uttered the unpardonable word. 'Well, de same day Mr Charles die, de same day Margaret go.' The look of triumph on Mable's face with open, glaring eyes and waving a warning right index finger, brought smiles to the Knowleses. But, their laughter was resounding when Mable added, 'As far as I concern, good riddance to bad rubbish!'

A brief, anticlimatic silence followed the emotional reunion. The event was a rare and unexpected one for Sandra, in view of her perception of her father's attitude towards black people. But Mable was special, she realised, and she, too, found herself being drawn to this loving and warm black woman. 'May I help you with breakfast, Mabes?'

'If you like, Miss Sandra.' Mable welcomed the offer, taking Sandra by the hand.

Betty embraced Bruce approvingly. 'I am proud of you, love.'

'What for?' Bruce blushed shyly.

'The way you treated Mable. She is black, remember?' Betty gave him a provocative glance.

'She is not black,' Bruce faltered. 'I mean, I know she's black, but, she's different.'

They both laughed at the apparent denial of the obvious, but in reality Bruce was expressing blackness not only as colour, but also as character.

Beatrice Andrews met the new family for the first time when she returned her breakfast tray to the kitchen. After the introductions Bruce asked her, 'How is uncle this morning?'

'Very much the same, sir. He should be up soon, if you wish to see him.'

Just then a car pulled into the driveway and soon Dr Korbinsky entered the house by the rear mud entrance, as usual. 'Good morning Bruce, Mrs Knowles and...' He paused to let Sandra introduce herself. 'I trust you had a pleasant journey home. It's good to have you back, Bruce.'

'Thank you, doctor,' Bruce replied. 'I was just this moment asking nurse about uncle's condition.'

'Let's go in, shall we?' Dr Korbinsky placed a gentle hand on Bruce's shoulder and led the family to Henry's room.

Nurse Andrews was already at Henry's side with file in hand. 'Morning doctor.'

'Morning Beatrice. How was he last night?' Dr Korbinsky was businesslike.

'A little restless, but he slept reasonably well.' She placed the file in the doctor's outstretched hand.

The doctor studied the charts and night reports slowly, punctuating each piece of information with a throaty grunt.

'Will he recover, doctor?' Bruce asked.

Dr Korbinsky hesitated before answering. 'Well, to be quite frank, it's a miracle your uncle is still alive. Few have survived cancer of this kind, at such an advanced stage, for so long. My unprofessional feeling is that he has been waiting to welcome you home.' He went on, stethoscope to ears, to examine Henry Knowles.

Betty drew close to Bruce as they both gazed at Henry. 'He looks so peaceful, Bruce. I hope he is not in pain.' Betty's whisper broke with emotion.

Dr Korbinsky completed his examination and gave instructions to Nurse Andrews. Then, he turned to Bruce and said, 'He

[47]

is weak, but, by early afternoon, he might be strong enough to communicate. His sight is totally gone. I expect he should leave us within the next twenty-four hours.'

A feeling of helplessness crept over Bruce. He approached his uncle, took hold of his lifeless hand and said, 'Well, uncle, I guess we all must go sometime. But don't you worry, I'm here to take care of things.' At this, Henry's trembling fingers curled around Bruce's, whose face lit up suddenly with excitement. 'Doc, I think he heard me. He is regaining strength, see?' Bruce showed Henry's clasp.

'You devil you, Henry!' Dr Korbinsky, too, was moved. 'You are certainly unpredictable.' He addressed Henry as if he were well again. 'I guess you are pleased that Bruce is here at last.'

A faint twitch of a smile disturbed the placidity of Henry's face, and everyone was smiling. But Dr Korbinsky broke out in joyous laughter which brought Mable running to the door. Huge glittering eyes peered at the unusual scene from the open door.

'Come on in, Mable,' Dr Korbinsky beckoned. 'Mr Henry is smiling for a change.'

'Praise God!' Mable rushed to the bedside with tear-filled eyes. 'Alleluiah! Fank you, Jesus!' Mable knelt by the bed praising and thanking God for that moment of joy. Nurse Beatrice wiped her tears as did Betty and Sandra.

But, alas, Henry's hand relaxed its grip of Bruce's. His smile began to fade slowly as his jaw sank to his chest.

'Doc!' Bruce called, 'I think he is going.'

'No!' Mable shouted. 'No!' Her agony pierced the stillness of the room.

A tense and profoundly quiet moment followed while Dr Korbinsky probed Henry's body for vital signs. Finally, he straightened up, turned to Bruce and said, 'I'm sorry, Bruce, he has left us.'

Mable stormed out of the room wailing. Bruce clenched his teeth to restrain his tears, but, for Sandra, Betty and Nurse Andrews tears of joy turned into tears of sorrow.

Dr Korbinsky sat at the table, pulled out a pad from his case and completed a death certificate. 'What a way to go,' he muttered. 'What a way to go.'

CHAPTER SIX

NEWS OF THE death of Henry Knowles spread like wildfire. Mourners from all over the island trekked their way to Knowles Gardens to pay their last respects. Henry's body, clothed in a sparkling white gabardine suit and black tie, lay serenely on satin sheets edged with gold braiding which matched the pillowcase on which his head rested. There was a faint smile on his face. The Caribbean sun splashed its dazzling brilliance everywhere in the room, and, with the smell of roses and carnations, a deathly atmosphere of peace and tranquility prevailed.

'He was a good man,' Mother Rosa was comforting Betty and Sandra. 'He was loved by everyone he knew.'

'You know, Mother, I wish I had known him when he was alive,' Betty lamented. 'Judging by the numbers who have passed through here, with tears in their eyes, I feel Dominica has lost a great soul.'

'You are absolutely right, Mrs Knowles.' Bishop Moore joined the group. 'How do you do, Madame? I am Bishop Moore. Please accept my condolences on behalf of the Church and parish.'

'Thank you, Your Excellency.' Betty was taken by surprise.

'I welcome you and your family to Dominica and our parish.' The bishop was awkwardly formal.

Betty introduced Sandra, who curtsied shyly. She added, 'My husband is in the office with Mr Johnson.'

'I would like to meet him to discuss funeral arrangements for tomorrow.'

'I'm sure he wouldn't want to miss you. Sandra will take you to him.' Betty touched Sandra's shoulder, and the bishop excused himself.

Bishop Moore returned every courtesy he received from mourners as he followed Sandra to the office. Sandra knocked on the door and opened it. 'Daddy, the bishop is here to see you.'

Bruce and Clifford stood when the bishop entered. 'Hello, Your Excellency,' Clifford greeted. 'Bruce Knowles,' he introduced.

Sandra closed the door and stood for a moment watching the crowd enter and leave Henry's room. She was overwhelmed by the atmosphere of grief and could feel her own sadness welling up within. 'How silly of me,' she murmured. 'I hardly knew the man.' But Sandra could no longer restrain her tears and quietly slipped outside near the swimming pool, taking refuge under a soursop tree.

She was as confused as she was sad. The experiences of death and bereavement were new to her. She felt more sorry for the mourners than for the loss of her grand-uncle. She was leaning against the fruit tree with eyes closed, when she heard someone sigh. She turned and saw Mable sitting on a bench rocking her body forward and backward, as if to lull her pain. Instantly, her tears began to flow once more. She rushed to Mable's side, crying, 'Oh, Mable, I'm sorry.'

Mable did not respond, but continued to finger the beads of her rosary in prayer. Her face was tear-stained and placid, her eyes open, yet vacant.

'Mable,' Sandra called softly, holding her arm. 'Mable,' she repeated when there was no answer. A feeling of horror came over Sandra. She shook Mable violently, but her response was only a faint smile as she continued her rocking and praying. 'Oh, my God!' Sandra breathed and ran into the house. She met Eugene leaving Henry's room, grabbed his hand, crying, 'Come, Eugene, something is the matter with Mable! She is just sitting outside saying nothing. She looks ill.' Sandra pulled him to the rear of the house.

He ran to the bench, calling, 'Mabes.' She continued her silent ritual. 'Come on, Mabes,' Eugene coaxed, 'it's all right, everything is okay.' But Mable only smiled faintly. He turned to Sandra 'She is in a state of shock. Help me take her to the car. She must see a doctor immediately.'

'I would consider it a great honour to read the eulogy, Your Excellency.' Clifford Johnson was pleased. 'The Knowles are like family to me.'

'Thank you, Clifford,' Bruce smiled, 'I've been away so long, I hardly qualify.'

'Well, that settles it.' Bishop Moore stood. 'The ceremony begins at three. There will be a High Mass, with Communion and choir. Henry deserves the best.'

'Thank you, Your Excellency,' Bruce opened the door and shook the bishop's hand in gratitude. Bruce and Clifford followed after the bishop and met Betty and Sandra.

'What's the matter Betty, you look worried.' Betty's face was tense with anxiety.

'It's Mable. She was taken to the hospital suffering from shock, Eugene believes.'

'I found her outside sitting on a bench, dad, just rocking herself and saying nothing,' Sandra explained.

'Poor Mabes,' Clifford shook his head in sorrow, 'she has suffered so much grief in this family. With the passing of Henry, she has lost everyone dearest to her.'

'I wouldn't say so, Clifford,' Bruce disagreed. 'She's got me and Betty and Sandra.' Bruce paused to smile at the questioning look on Clifford's face. 'Yes, Cliff, Mabes is very dear to me, but you probably wouldn't know how much. Someday I'll explain.'

Clifford's curiosity turned into a cheerful smile. Had time healed the wounds of hatred and prejudice in Bruce? Could Dr Korbinsky be right?

It was two hours later, as the final group of mourners bade goodbye to Bruce and family, when Eugene and Mable returned, followed by Dr Korbinsky.

Bruce hurried to her. 'Are you all right, now, Mabes?' He placed his arm around her waist and led her to the living room couch.

'I awright, Brucie,' she said softly, 'I on'y a little tired, doctor say.'

Clifford and Dr Korbinsky eyed each other and smiled approvingly. But Eugene gazed, spellbound, upon the show of affection and concern from Bruce Knowles. Then, Eugene smiled and thought, 'Maybe I was wrong'.

'So, how is she, doc?' Bruce asked.

'She needs immediate rest. The events of the last two days were more than she could withstand emotionally,' Dr Korbinsky explained. 'After a good rest, she will be on her feet again.'

'Come, let me take you to your room, Betty and Bruce helped Mable up. 'You've been on your feet ever since we arrived. San and I will take care of the house while you rest.'

'No, mam!' Mable objected. 'I get somebody to help. A good frien' of mine a'ks for a job here. She comin' right away.'

'Well, I don't know,' Betty hesitated, looking at her husband for approval.

'I think we will need an extra hand, Betty, don't you?' Bruce approved. 'There will be more work from now on, and Mabes needs help.'

'I guess, so,' Betty agreed. 'Would you call your friend Mable?'

'Yes, mam.' She turned to Eugene. 'Eugie, you know Janet on Baff Road?' Eugene shrugged ignorance. 'You know Janet, man, who have a chil' for Vantille. She stayin' wif her modder on Baff Road, near de convent gate.'

'Oh, yes,' Eugene remembered. 'Janet Bardouille.'

'Right. Go an' tell her to come an' work here right now.'

He left promptly, still wondering at the turn of events at Knowles Gardens, and in particular, with Bruce Knowles' change of attitude.

'Come on Mable, it's time for your rest.' Betty took her hand.

'Yes, mam. But I have to light Mr Henry candle first,' she insisted.

'I'll help you, Mable,' Sandra followed.

Betty turned to Clifford and Dr Korbinsky with palms upward to show her lack of understanding of Mable's obsession.

'It's the custom to keep a light burning for the dead until nine nights following burial,' Clifford explained. 'Friends of the family keep vigil in prayers and song. The ninth night is a joyous occasion.'

Dr Korbinsky nodded 'we are a very traditional and religious people in Dominica.'

'I need a drink.' Bruce walked into the bar. 'Would you gentlemen care to join me?' Clifford and the doctor followed and mounted stools while Bruce fetched the glasses and rum punch.

Betty excused herself to join Mable and Sandra in Henry's room. Mable was straightening the silver crucifix which stood prominently on the only table. It was flanked on either side by two silver candlesticks. The flames from the candles wavered gently in the air movement created by Mable's activity. She rearranged the roses and carnations at the bedside, then stopped to look upon the ashen face of her former master. 'Well, Mr Henry, you boun' to go to Heaven. God know what He doin'.' She spoke as if Henry would understand.

Betty joined her at the bedside. 'He must have been a very kind man,' she added.

'I goin' to miss him, Mrs Brucie,' Mable confessed as she straightened his starched, white collar. She recoiled slightly when her hand touched his cold chin. Mable sighed, looked around the room, drew the curtain, and said, 'Now, Mr Henry can res' in peace.' She crossed herself, prayerfully, leaving the door wide open when they departed.

'I'm certainly pleased to see you here to take over the business, Bruce. I dreaded the thought of Riversdale Plantations falling into the hands of inept civil servants who pretend to be agriculturalists.' Clifford was on his second glass of punch, as were Bruce and Dr Korbinsky. 'We need strong, tenacious leadership to manage workers in Dominica. An apathetic attitude to work prevails in this rich and beautiful island. If only the people would realise what a blessed country this is, oh, what paradise!' Clifford lamented.

'I share your sentiments, Cliff.' Dr Korbinsky licked his lips in obvious enjoyment of the citric kick from the punch. 'However, Charles and Henry were both very fair with the plantation workers. Their loyalty to Charles and Henry went far beyond satisfactory conditions of work and adequate wages. They regarded them as old colonial masters, who not only sustained their families, but also helped them above and beyond the call of duty, as benevolent overlords.'

Bruce smiled at Clifford and the doctor as they showered praises upon the dead. Were they trying to say something to him? Or, were they just being kind at this hour of grief? Bruce knew very little about his father and uncle. But he could not understand how his father could have commanded respect from black people if he went to bed with their women. Bruce winced as the thought occurred to him.

'Yes, Bruce, you certainly have a tough act to follow.' Clifford misread Bruce's facial expression. He drained his glass of the last drop of punch and looked at his watch. 'I guess I can manage one for the road.'

Bruce helped Clifford and himself to more rum punch. 'Yes, a tough act to follow,' he acknowledged, 'but if my father and uncle did it, I guess I can.'

'That's the spirit!' Clifford raised his glass to toast his approval.

'In fact,' Bruce continued, 'not only I can, but I must,' he emphasised. 'I will not stand for any laziness, any pilfering or any rudeness from subordinates.' Bruce paused, but paid little heed to the silence and raised eyebrows of his colleagues. 'By the sweat and blood of my father and uncle Riversdale Plantations is what it is today. I'll be damned if I let it fall into the grabbing hands of politicians.' He turned to the others for approval.

Dr Korbinsky recognised the glitter of oncoming inebriation in Bruce's eyes. 'You are quite right,' he said calmly, 'a tough approach is advisable to begin with. And when this is clearly established, continued respect can be reinforced by fair and equitable treatment of workers. Mind you,' he raised a warning finger, 'an iron hand smacks of the old and detestable days of slavery. Today, Dominicans do not take kindly to that type of domination, and many a plantation have fallen because colonial overlords failed to appreciate the new liberation.'

'Yes, indeed!' Clifford was visibly stimulated by the discussion. 'It is to the credit of your father, Charles, when he placed Eugene as the direct supervisor over the workers. Eugene was a timely catalyst during the uprising among plantation workers three years ago. Henry criticised your father for breaking the tradition of white management, but results have proved that he was far-sighted and responsive to changing trends.'

'Very well said, Cliff,' Dr Korbinsky stepped in. 'And, what was even more surprising, Bruce, Eugene is a respected and popular trade unionist. That fact, in my estimation, helped Riversdale Plantations to survive the turbulent times.'

Bruce listened with wandering attention. Several questions came to mind, questions he could not ask his colleagues. He had to see for himself. For instance, in that situation, how much control did his father and uncle really have over the workers? Could a trade unionist be trusted to manage workers in the best interest of Riversdale? How much power did Eugene wield in the affairs of Riversdale? Above all, can a black man really take charge, or was Eugene just a token gesture to appease restless workers?

Clifford stood up. 'It's time to go. You've got a busy day ahead of you.'

'Indeed yes,' Dr Korbinsky followed.

Bruce escorted them to the door.

'You can count on my continued support, Bruce,' Clifford assured him. 'I consider myself family. Charles and Henry were my two closest friends. They would expect me to assist you whenever you ask.'

'I appreciate that, Cliff, especially as I am new at it,' Bruce thanked.

'However, you can depend on Eugene. His knowledge in the business is second to none,' Clifford added.

[57]

'By the way,' Dr Korbinsky remembered, 'I expect we'll be seeing you at the Red Rose Club. That's our usual meeting place.'

'I'd love to, doctor,' Bruce agreed.

'Henry, call me Henry.' Dr Korbinsky waved goodbye as did Clifford.

Bruce stood at the door watching the men drive away. While there, he saw Eugene returning with the new domestic worker. He watched them enter the kitchen doorway, then approached them.

'Good afternoon, sir.' Janet was soft spoken, her voice betraying her timidity.

'Good evening,' Bruce was curt.

'I'm Janet, the maid Mable sen' for.' Janet forced a smile to hide her fear of the penetrating stare from Bruce Knowles.

'Just wait here. I'll get Mrs Knowles.' Bruce left.

As soon as he was out of hearing, Janet turned anxiously to Eugene and whispered, 'Bon dieu! I don' like dis man at all. I not stayin'. No sir!' Janet turned to leave.

Eugene laughed. 'Since when you 'fraid, man?' He teased. 'He is a pussy cat compared with Vantille.'

Janet laughed at the comment and felt relaxed. 'You right. As long as dey pay me well, I don' care. Besides, is Mable dat sen' for me, not no white man.'

Just then, Bruce returned with Betty. Betty smiled pleasantly, and stretched a hand in welcome. 'Hello, Janet. We are glad you could come. Mable said you are a good worker and recommended you for a job. Come, let me take you to Mable. She's not feeling too well and doctor ordered her to rest a while.'

Bruce looked at Janet as she passed him. She was neither white nor black, more apricot coloured. Her hair was not like Mable's, thick, curly and black, but dark brown, wavy and falling to her shoulders. Her eyes were light brown and glowed in the early evening light. Bruce sulked at the sudden memory of Simone's joke back in London about those sexy, black girls.

'Well, sir, I'm leaving now.' Eugene was still standing at the kitchen entrance.

[58]

'Oh, Eugene,' Bruce said abruptly, 'I want to talk with you before you leave.' They stepped into the living room. 'I'll be making a tour of the estate on Monday after lunch. Mr Johnson will be with me. Let the workers know I'll be talking to them. I understand that you were placed in this job three years ago because plantation workers were agitating for more wages and better conditions. I also understand that you've done a very good job, so far. But, that remains to be seen.' Bruce smiled dryly. 'It is my intention to see to it that Riversdale continues to be a profitable business. I know, from experience in England, that you people tend to be lazy and have to be driven constantly to produce. It goes without saying, this won't be tolerated.'

Eugene was taken by surprise. The muscles of his stomach tightened, a physical reaction of one who tries to protect himself from the unexpected blow below the belt. He breathed deeply, but remained silent as Bruce Knowles continued.

'Of course, you'll appreciate that as a novice in the business I will need your full assistance for the first few weeks.' Bruce looked at Eugene for some reply, but, there was none. 'Do not think for one moment that I will be dependent on you. You may as well know I trust no one, for man is by nature corrupt and self-seeking. We all do what we do for our own ends.' He paused to pick up his pipe at the bar and began to remove the ashes.

Eugene looked at his new boss curiously, whose hands were shaking uneasily as he poked at the hardened, charred tobacco. He did not know what to think of Bruce's speech. He would have liked to probe the mind of this stranger, for such Bruce really was. But Eugene chose silence at this first encounter, and was relieved when Bruce concluded.

'I guess this is all I have to say at this point. I hope we understand each other clearly. Riversdale Plantations will come first in all my dealings. What's good for the plantation must be good for the workers, for, without Riversdale Plantations there will be a lot of empty bellies.'

'I understand,' Eugene hastened to say. 'I will alert the workers about your visit.' He dismissed himself without another word and without bidding Bruce goodnight. Bruce watched him go, equally silent.

As Eugene drove away from Knowles Gardens, he tried to understand the true message Bruce was conveying to him. To begin with, it was a totally negative one. He referred to black people as lazy, the very stereotype past slave masters used as justification for whipping slaves. He said that Riversdale was feeding hungry, empty bellies. This meant that the workers were totally dependent on Riversdale for their survival, another strategy of control utilised by slave masters. The more Eugene thought about it, the more it became clear to him that Bruce hated black people.

'And why did he imply that he didn't trust me?' Eugene mused. 'Why? Am I a threat to him? His uncle placed his total trust in me, and Mr Johnson confided that were it not for me the Plantations might have suffered the same disaster as most other colonial estates.'

Eugene was so deep in thought that he had to stamp the brakes hard to avoid collision with an approaching jeep. 'Damn you, Bruce Knowles!' He shouted. 'What right have you got to talk to me like that?' He turned east from Queen Mary Street on to Great Marlborough Street and parked behind the huge concrete step to his home. He did not see Monique standing on the porch. He slammed the door of the car angrily.

Monique was startled. 'Hey, Euge, what's eating you?' she greeted, moving aside from the entrance to let him in.

'That white son-of-a-gun, Bruce Knowles, has just shown me his true colours.' Eugene walked directly to the kitchen to pour himself a tall glass of rum packed with ice cubes. 'I tell you, Nicky, if I didn't have respect for the dead, Bruce Knowles wouldn't have known what hit him!'

'What happened? What did he do?' Monique's adrenalin began to rise in empathy. 'Did he touch you?'

'Touch me?' Eugene laughed out heartily. They both laughed, and, for a brief moment Monique buried her body into his to kiss his moist neck. But, Eugene was in no mood for caressing.

'Nicky, you know how hard I've worked to make the Plantation one of the best on the island. The workers trust me completely and we never lost a worker during the uprising, remember?' There was a note of sadness in his voice.

Monique nodded a silent reply as she looked into Eugene's eyes. His pain was deep, she could tell from the conviction with which he spoke.

'You know, Henry Knowles didn't get the MBE for nothing. He got it for the contribution Riversdale Plantation made to the economy of the island, and to agriculture in particular.' Eugene knew, only too well, that he was the driving force behind this honourable recognition. In fact, Henry Knowles acknowledged that when he spoke to the workers. 'It was your doing, not mine,' Henry had said. 'And we must congratulate Eugene for his indefatigable persistence in making it possible for us.'

'We were a great team, Nicky, just like one big family who had one another's welfare at heart,' Eugene smiled pleasantly, and so did Monique.

'And I'm sure you will continue to be a great team, Eugie,' Monique encouraged.

'I'm not so sure, Nicky. I'm not so sure.' Eugene's voice faded as doubt about the future of Riversdale rose before him.

'So, what happened between you and this Bruce Knowles?'

'Who knows?' Eugene shrugged his shoulders. 'From the way he spoke to me tonight, it seems very clear to me he doesn't like us blacks.'

'Really!' Monique drawled sarcastically.

'Well, he doesn't. The man had the audacity to say, to my face, that black people are lazy, have to be forced to work, that he doesn't trust us, and the estate is feeding our hungry, empty stomachs.' Eugene smiled.

'He said that!' Nicky looked at her husband in disbelief.

'Oh yes, he did. And more,' Eugene added.

'What else?'

'This one is a surprise, Nicky, and I thought I had heard the last of it. But no. You remember what the boys in the Union said when I took the job three years ago?'

'Well, I know they felt you made a mistake taking the job.

And, oh yes, some of them even called you a traitor because you were not going to help the strike they were planning. Isn't that right?' Monique remembered.

'Yes,' Eugene confirmed, 'and some called me the white man's puppet. That they gave me the job so the workers would feel they had a black man on their side who would look after their welfare.'

'That's right, and so you did,' Monique emphasised. 'Everybody is trying to get work at Riversdale because the pay is the best in the island. So the Union was wrong.'

'They were wrong because I proved them wrong, Nicky,' Eugene said with a triumphant look on his face. 'They could have been right if I were interested only in myself. But they didn't know that Henry Knowles was genuinely interested in the workers, too. That is what really made me take the job. Henry Knowles proved to be a man of his word up to his death.' Eugene paused, then added respectfully, 'May his soul rest in peace.'

'Amen,' Monique answered likewise.

A moment of silence followed before Eugene got up to refill his glass. 'Shall I mix you one?' He asked Monique.

'No thanks,' she replied. 'But I want to know what else happened between you and Bruce.'

'Well, as I was saying,' Eugene continued, 'Bruce Knowles came up with this same old story that the Union was broadcasting about me. He told me he understood his father hired me because the workers were agitating for more wages and better conditions.'

'What!' Monique exclaimed with surprise. 'So, he thinks you are a puppet too?'

'I couldn't believe I was hearing him right. But that's what he said. I tell you, Nicky, that hurt me, you know.' Eugene shook his head in disbelief. 'I was boiling inside to tell Bruce to go to hell, but I kept my cool. I have too much respect for the dead.'

'De man jus' come to dis country an' he start bodderin' people awready!' Monique sank into colloquialism. 'Well, *crapaud* smoke his pipe!'

This saying brought fits of laughter from Eugene while he observed, 'And he smokes a pipe as well.' Their laughter was resounding.

CHAPTER SEVEN

THE ROSEAU cathedral was packed to its limit. Hundreds of mourners gathered for the burial service of Henry Knowles. The bell began to toll its mournful monotones, signalling the approaching procession. Three acolytes were busy preparing the altar, while the organ bellowed a sad refrain.

On the narrow winding road through the Botanic Gardens the procession snailed its way. The tall saaman trees which lined the route swayed farewell to Henry Knowles in a picturesque and fitting guard of honour. Henry Knowles had admired the Gardens as his own. He loved to stroll there in the early evening with his wife, Maria, when the huge trees cast their long shadows against the golden light of the setting sun. Hand in hand, they would stop to chat with strollers, or just to admire some exotic plant or flower which sprang there in controlled profusion.

But, now, it was adieu to Henry Knowles as the hearse made its exit at the western gate of the Gardens. Even then, some mourners had not yet left Knowles Gardens a quarter mile away. An elderly grey-haired man, standing on the sidewalk, cane in one hand and straw hat in the other, bowed his head in respect as the hearse passed by. On each side of the hearse were three pall-bearers, among them Eugene St Rose and Samuel Harris. Immediately following the hearse were Bruce, Betty, and Sandra, the only three surviving relatives of Henry Knowles.

Bruce grimaced in the heat of the afternoon sun. His dark jacket hugged his shoulders tightly, disclosing its age and lack of use. His fingers were clasped in reverse position behind his back, while his gaze remained fixed on the hearse before him. But he strode easily and steadily.

Sandra wore a black veil of silk lace over her head, partly covering her face. Her youthful beauty, however, defied concealment. She held a faint smile while her eyes darted about with unabashed curiosity.

Betty Knowles was a picture of elegance. Her auburn hair glittered beneath the dark lace which fell gracefully upon her breast. She wore dark skirt and jacket beneath which a white chiffon blouse displayed intricate embroidery. A necklace of cultured pearls adorned her neck. She graced the procession, unmindful it seemed, of the blazing torment of the tropical sun.

Bishop Moore stood with two priests and three acolytes awaiting the arrival of the procession.

Inside the cathedral the organ moaned a soothing, solemn 'Nearer My God To Thee', which matched the stolid faces of the congregation.

An impressive Catholic High Mass was sung, highlighted by an eulogy from Clifford Johnson. He was gracious in his delivery, his voice breaking with emotion when he said, 'Henry was like a brother to me, and I feel I've lost my best friend.' He echoed the sentiments of many a Dominican, black as well as white. 'He was a man,' Clifford continued, 'who would stop at nothing to give a helping hand to those in need.'

This last quality described the true character of Henry Knowles in a nutshell. This was the secret of his success, the willingness to share with others and expect nothing in return. Several heads nodded their approval of this fact, not least of all, His Honour the Administrator and Queen's representative, Sir Humphrey Codrington.

But it was the raspy death tones of the 'Libera Me', chanting in a tired, forlorn, solemn rendition, which pierced the hearts of the congregation. Handkerchiefs dabbed eyes too difficult to restrain tears, and none could disallow the agony which Mable poured forth, unashamedly, at this final farewell at the cemetery. Bruce

[66]

Knowles maintained his composure throughout the ceremony. During the laying of wreaths and flowers, he was able to smile with all who wished his family well, and was particularly pleased to meet Sir Humphrey and Lady Codrington.

'Your uncle was a fine man of this soil. We shall miss him very much,' Sir Humphrey praised as he shook hands with Bruce and family. 'Please accept condolences on behalf of Her Majesty.'

'We thank you very much, your Honour, and please convey our gratitude to Her Majesty,' Bruce reciprocated.

Lady Codrington expressed a desire to meet the family again under happier circumstances, to which Betty replied, 'We shall look forward to it, Your Ladyship, and, thank you for honouring us with your presence.'

Clifford introduced the Premier of the island. 'Bruce, the Premier, Mr John St Luce.'

'How do you do, sir?' Bruce stretched a hand to the black political leader.

'It's a pleasure to meet you Mr Knowles, Mrs Knowles and Miss Knowles, I assume? The Premier smiled. 'Henry is a great loss to us. He was a true friend to Government, and was quick to give advice, even without our asking. He played a major role in the formulation of our present policy on agriculture. I assure you, Mr Knowles, the people of Dominica owe him much. We in Government will do our best to ensure that you, as his heir and your family enjoy the same respect and good fortune Henry enjoyed. Don't hesitate to call on us if you feel the need. And, good luck to you and your family.'

'Thank you, Mr Premier,' Bruce accepted calmly.

'Please call me John.' The Premier was informal. 'Premier means first, but, in truth, the people come first.' He smiled and waved goodbye.

'Not a bad chap,' Bruce remarked to Clifford.

'Don't be fooled by his charm, Bruce,' Clifford raised a warning eyebrow. 'That's his secret. He is always campaigning.'

Dr Korbinsky approached Bruce and family accompanied by a white family. 'Please meet the Radcliffes, Errol, Martha, and son, Mark.'

Mark's hand was moist and cold despite the warm weather. But Sandra could not hide her delight at meeting someone of her generation. 'Hello.' She was apprehensive, but looked him straight in the eye.

'Hi, please to meet you.' His voice was more youthful than his rugged features and deep-set eyes would indicate. He stood at least six feet. 'I guess you came for the funeral, eh?' His English accent had acquired the creole rhythm of the Caribbean.

Sandra smiled at the music in his voice. 'Oh no, we're here to stay, at least for a while.'

'Nice,' Mark sang, 'I hope we become friends.'

'I hope so, too,' Sandra heard herself say.

The crowd dwindled slowly as the last wreaths and flowers were laid on the grave. Bruce was the last to lay his wreath, saying, 'Well, uncle, you have left me a legacy, not only of wealth, but of friendship, power and a good name in the community. I swear, upon your grave, I'll defend the good name of this family with all my might.'

Samuel closed the car door and sat heavily beside Eugene. 'Boy, I'm glad it's over,' he sighed, yanking off his tie.

'Well, my friend, there is more to come,' Eugene smiled provocatively as he started the car. 'You haven't heard anything yet.'

'What do you mean?' Samuel did not like the tone of Eugene's voice. He knew him well enough to recognise when he was worried. He had listened to many speeches from Eugene at trade union meetings, and sensed that something was wrong. It was the introductory phrase, 'my friend', that alerted him. This was how Eugene always addressed his audience.

'I need a drink right now,' Eugene said. 'Let's stop at the Royal Saloon.'

Samuel hesitated. 'I don't have enough cash.'

'Don't worry, Sam. The drinks are on me. Besides, you accountants never have enough cash, anyway!' They laughed at the pun.

'Okay, I'm game if you're buying,' Samuel agreed. 'So what's up?' he probed.

'You know, I think I've done a pretty good job at Riversdale, wouldn't you say?'

'There's no denying that. The records are there to prove it,' Samuel confirmed. 'If anyone knows, I should.'

'Would you say I took the job at Riversdale for purely selfish ends?' Eugene asked.

'That could hardly be said, Euge, considering the number of hours you put into it.' Samuel was honest. 'Most overseers leave the nurturing to nature, as Henry would say. But, not you. Nature can be destructive as well as creative. Man must work with nature to protect the good fruits and weed out the bad. I know you follow that creed.'

Eugene turned to Samuel and smiled. 'You have missed your true vocation, Sam. You should have been at Riversdale instead of me.'

'Oh, no. I learnt that from you.'

'From me?' Eugene tried to recall.

'From one of your talks with students. Remember when you were asked by the Banana Association to lecture on Leaf Spot Control?' Samuel stirred Eugene's memory.

'Oh, yes. That was nearly two years ago. The disease was becoming an epidemic and we had to arrest it as quickly as possible.' Eugene laughed. 'Now, isn't it ironic, that today we have the new problem of eradicating the misuse of the preventive chemical agent?'

'Anyway,' Samuel interrupted Eugene's reminiscence, 'you succeeded in your efforts with nature and we saved the major part of our banana crop the following year. Now, tell me what the hell is bothering you!'

Eugene parked the car, and the two men entered the saloon. 'Two pissy colds, Jim, and keep them coming.' Eugene ordered Caribbean beer. They removed their jackets and hung them at the back of their chairs. 'Look, Sam,' Eugene began, 'I don't know what to make of it, but our new boss had a chat with me last night . . . not a chat, it was more like a lecture, which made my blood boil.'

'Oh, yeah!' Samuel gave Eugene his undivided attention even though the bartender had placed the drinks before them.

[69]

'Yep!' Eugene replied. 'To make a long story short, Bruce said to my face that black people are lazy and cannot be trusted.'

'You're joking!' Samuel's response was immediate.

'No, Sam. No joke.'

'But what is this!' Samuel became offended. 'Was he drunk or something?'

'No.' Eugene took a long gulp from the sweating mug of ice-cold beer. He exhaled heartily as the coldness radiated through his hot body. He saw the fury in Samuel's eyes and immediately knew why. 'Sam, you hold the key to the piggy bank of Riversdale Plantations. If anyone should be trusted completely it should be you.'

'This is exactly what crossed my mind.'

'Imagine Bruce Knowles looking you in the face and telling you he doesn't trust you, what would be your reaction?' Eugene took another mouthful, almost emptying the mug.

Now, it was Samuel's turn to soothe his rising temperature. He almost emptied the mug with his first quenching. Unlike Eugene, he gave no physical sign of enjoyment. But, he smiled when his eyes met Eugene's. Samuel was a man of integrity. He had served the business faithfully for the past eight years. The question of trust had never arisen either with Charles or Henry Knowles. On what basis, then, could a newcomer like Bruce Knowles declare a lack of trust in him?

'I would demand an apology,' Samuel said calmly, 'or I would make him pay for his tongue!'

Eugene smiled. Two more beers were placed on the table. He slowly topped his mug, gazing at the froth rising in an effervescent dome. 'You know, Sam,' Eugene continued softly, 'Bruce Knowles hates black people.'

Samuel looked at Eugene with a big grin, as if he had heard the joke of the day.

Eugene expected this dubious reaction from Samuel. 'It is true, Sam. One day I'll tell you the whole story because Mabes wouldn't lie. She loves him very much, which is part of the story.'

Samuel's attention was now focused on Eugene's revelations. For the moment, the beers were forgotten. 'Can't you just give me a brief summary of the story? I'm curious,' Samuel begged.

'Okay. In a nutshell, soon after his mother died, when Bruce was a kid, he caught his father making love to one of the black servants. He became so infuriated that he ran away from home. Mable found him by the water pipe up the river. He told her what happened, and for three years he confided only in her till he was sent to England, presumably for schooling. Since then he has hated black people.'

'Does that make sense,' Samuel asked, 'confiding in Mable, who is black?'

'Well, he was just a kid,' Eugene suggested. 'In any case, Mable was only, what, nineteen years old at the time? I think Bruce was hurt, and no one but Mable comforted him. Instead, they shipped him to England which left the unresolved hurt to fester all these years.'

'So he has returned to pay back, is that it?' Samuel deduced.

'So it seems,' Eugene agreed, 'and from what he said to me, he means business.' Eugene laughed. 'He said a lot more to me, Sam, which I don't care to talk about right now. But I can see big trouble ahead for Riversdale.'

CHAPTER EIGHT

B RUCE KNOWLES was fascinated throughout the drive to Riversdale Plantations. The journey held no more excitement for Clifford Johnson who had travelled it hundreds of times before with the Knowles brothers. But for Bruce, who could not recall his boyhood experiences, driving the narrow and sinuous road cut along the mountain side was a death-defying adventure.

Bruce held his breath at every bend, where sheer precipices gape at you with jagged ferocity. Yet, the undulating plains below, intersected by evergreen valleys and meandering rivulets, invite you to sojourn in the bosom of nature's serenity. It is this unique contradiction of ruggedness and beauty that has earned the island the enviable name of Cinderella of the Caribbean.

'You've hardly said a word, Bruce. What's on your mind?' Clifford hated the silence while driving this lonely and treacherous mountain road.

'Oh, I was lost in the wonder of nature,' Bruce welcomed the diversion. 'This is, indeed, beautiful country.'

'None more beautiful,' Clifford echoed.

'You know,' Bruce continued, 'I often wondered what madness drives the people of the Caribbean to abandon their sunshine paradises for the dreary cities of Europe and North America.'

'Opportunity,' Clifford suggested. 'The people want the chance to achieve the goals and fulfil the ambitions that colonial education tells them are important in life.'

'And what are these, may I ask?' Bruce laughed.

'The same ones you pursue, Bruce. Wealth, a home of your own to raise a family, higher education to enhance employment opportunity, the luxuries of life like a car, and generally, a better standard of living.'

'This is not what they are doing in England, I assure you.' Bruce was emphatic. 'They are a constant embarrassment to the British people. The crime rate has increased because of their presence, racial tension is at its highest ever, and now London and Birmingham have their ghettos. I tell you, Clifford, these people would be better off in their own countries.'

Clifford hesitated before replying to what he considered was an embellishment of the facts. He would not say outright that Bruce was wrong, but he felt the compulsion to let him know that people in the Caribbean are not ignorant of the world situation. 'You know, Bruce,' Clifford chose his words carefully, 'the conditions and events which you describe in England occur everywhere, even here in Dominica. We read about them daily in the newspapers. But these conditions and events do not tell the full story, as you will appreciate.'

Bruce Knowles nodded acknowledgement when Clifford alluded to his sense of appreciation.

'England has one of the lowest crime rates in the world,' Clifford continued, 'and this rate has been relatively constant for the past decade.'

Bruce nodded agreement.

'Mind you, I believe it is possible to reduce the crime rate in England to the level in the Caribbean,' Clifford concluded.

Bruce narrowed his eyes in disbelief. He could have questioned Clifford's comparison, but what if he were correct? He hesitated.

Clifford smiled. He knew, from experience, that he had planted reasonable doubt in Bruce's mind to let his argument go unchallenged. He broke the silence once more. 'But you are right, Bruce, this is beautiful country. I wouldn't part with it for all the wealth in the world.' He touched Bruce, and pointed. 'Riversdale Plantations extends from here, down the valley, across the banana and citrus groves, up the hills into the coffee plantations. Again, up the other valley where the river flows and right across back to the base of this mountain. This is your inheritance, Bruce, three hundred and forty acres of first grade agricultural land.'

There was a lingering smile on Bruce's face as the jeep descended into the valley. Already, he could see signs of human activity here and there. As the jeep approached Riversdale House, four large dogs rose from their basking in the sun to welcome the visitors. Their growling alerted Eugene who emerged from the nursery.

'Hi, Eugene,' Clifford greeted.

'Hi,' Eugene waved. 'That way,' he pointed to Riversdale House. 'I'm coming just now.'

Bruce followed Clifford to the house where Eugene joined them moments later. Already, Bruce and Clifford were being refreshed by coconut water, one of nature's most thirst-quenching, unadulterated beverages. 'Have you told the workers about the meeting following lunch?' Bruce did not look in Eugene's direction.

'I have,' Eugene replied. 'We have an hour to spare. Would you like a tour of the plantations in the meantime?'

'There will be enough time for that. Is there some office where we can talk without interruptions? As overseer, I think you should be the first to know about my intentions.'

'Upstairs.' Eugene led the way, followed by Bruce and Clifford. A lizard sped across the wooden floor and disappeared through the open door leading to the verandah overlooking the access road.

Bruce stepped onto the verandah to enjoy the view. 'That's perfect,' he observed, looking down at the lawn below. 'Eugene, let the workers assemble on the lawn. I will address them from here.'

Sandra was pleased to learn that Mother Rosa taught her English.

'She is the strictest nun in the whole bunch,' Debra was telling her. 'She doesn't get along well with most students because she is always moralising. I think she wants to make nuns of all of us.' They giggled.

[75]

Debra Henderson shared a twin desk with Sandra. She was astonishingly beautiful. Her dark long hair was held in a ponytail by a white ribbon, letting it fall loosely upon her back. She was light brown in complexion, and her features were neither caucasian nor negroid. Sandra was curious to know more about her, for she was different from the other black students. She might be East Indian, yet she was not, for she looked different from those Sandra knew in London.

'Where are you from?' Sandra asked.

'From Salybia,' Debra replied.

'Where is that?'

'Up north, on the Carib Reserve.' Debra smiled at the blank expression on Sandra's face. 'I am a Carib. You know, the original inhabitants of the Caribbean islands?' Debra explained, believing that Sandra had some knowledge of the history of the Caribbean.

'Really!' Sandra raised her voice as her curiosity mounted.

'Shh,' Debra whispered, placing her finger to her lips as Mother Rosa entered the classroom.

'Good afternoon, girls,' Mother Rosa greeted.

'Good afternoon, Mother,' the class dragged its chorus.

Mother Rosa surveyed the faces before her. Her black-rimmed spectacles sat firmly on her nose, making an impression on the sides of her face. She smiled when she saw Sandra. 'Welcome, Sandra. I hope you enjoy the rest of the term with us. You will find the change from England to Dominica is not much since we write examinations set by the University of Cambridge. Your curriculum will be changed only slightly, but, from your school records, we think you will be ready for the upcoming exams.'

For a brief moment, Sandra was the centre of attention until Mother Rosa turned abruptly to the blackboard and scratched, 'Structure of a Good Essay'.

Betty picked up the telephone. 'Hi, dear,' Bruce greeted, 'Clifford and I are at the Red Rose for lunch.'

'You didn't stay long on the estate.'

[76]

'It was a short meeting,' Bruce began to say, then added hesitatingly, 'in fact, it ended sooner than expected. But, I'll explain when I get in this evening. How are things at home?'

'Fine. The gardeners are helping us move the furniture around as we discussed.'

'Good.' Bruce sounded distant.

'Did everything go all right at Riversdale?' Betty sensed his detachment.

'Well, not to my satisfaction. But I'll tell you all about it when I get home. Tah.' Bruce hung up, leaving his wife holding the receiver and staring blankly at Mable.

'Somefing wrong, mam?' Mable approached her.

'Oh, no Mable,' Betty replaced the receiver. 'Bruce called to say he was having lunch with Clifford at the Red Rose Club.'

'Red Rose Club!' Mable bellowed. 'So early in de afternoon?' She placed both hands on her hips to show her disapproval.

'Why? What's wrong with the Red Rose Club?' Betty became concerned.

'Noffing, mam,' Mable assured her, 'but every time Mr Charles and Mr Henry go to Red Rose dey comin' back drunk an' makin' trouble for Miss Maria an' Miss Bella.'

Betty laughed heartily, relieved that Mable's fears were no cause for alarm.

'You laughin' mam? You don' know what use to happen, non!' Mable did not share Betty's light-heartedness. 'One night, Mr Henry get so drunk, Mr Clifford have to drive him home. But, when he reach, is me he want to dance wif.' Mable sucked her teeth sulkingly. 'He chase me all aroun' de room, an' Miss Maria an' Mr Clifford only stay dere laughin'.' Mable paused to catch her breath as she recalled the incident with wild gesticulation.

Betty was grinning from ear to ear as she pictured this huge black woman being pursued by a helpless, drunken, white man. 'So, what happened?'

'Well, Mr Henry cetch me, but he so drunk, an' I so heavy, I loss my balance an' we fall on de centre table, an' dat is de en' of de centre table. It break in half! An' all of dem start to laugh as if

[77]

is a big joke.' Mable raised both hands like a maestro signalling a crescendo.

Betty's laughter was so joyous and hearty that tears filled her eyes. 'That was funny. So what did you do?'

'Well, I cry, because I so mad wif Mr Henry for makin' me break Miss Maria nice table.'

'You cried!' Betty was still laughing. 'You didn't break the table. Henry was more to blame. He was chasing you.'

'But he drunk,' Mable said painfully. 'I don' like to see dem drunk. Is always trouble. Like when Mr Charles go after Margaret?' Mable's countenance changed abruptly, as if reacting to a sudden pain. She realised she was introducing a subject better left dormant.

'Was she pretty?' Betty asked.

'Who, mam?' Mable looked at Betty with startled eyes.

'Margaret, Charles's woman?' Betty smiled. 'I know all about it. Bruce told me. Was she prettier than Bella?'

Mable did not answer the question, for her thoughts returned to the pain that young Bruce had suffered. 'Poor Brucie,' she sighed. 'Is Margaret fault, because she always waggin' like a dog when she see Mr Charles. She encourage him.'

'I wouldn't say that, Mable.' Betty shook her head. 'It takes two to tango.'

Mable looked at Betty and smiled. 'You right, Miss Betty. Mr Charles should have more respec' for Miss Bella. But, Margaret should know her place, too.'

The gardeners completed their tasks and approached Mable for their reward, a drink of rum. Betty grimaced when she saw the men drink the white rum in one swift gulp, chased by a mouthful of water.

'I think Mother Rosa likes you, Sandra.' Debra was walking part of the way home with Sandra, through the Botanic Gardens. 'Did you notice how she kept smiling to you when she looked into our direction?'

'I think she was smiling to you, Debie. Are you her favourite?' Sandra joked.

'Her favourite!' Debra laughed. 'Don't be surprised if she warns you about keeping company with me. They all think I am a wayward child.'

'Why?'

'Well,' Debra smiled shyly, 'I was seen talking to this boy from the Grammar School after mass one Sunday, and on Monday I was called to Mother Superior's office and given a long lecture on how I was giving the school a bad name, and things like that.'

'Just because you were talking to a boy?' Sandra asked with disbelief.

'Well he was holding my hand,' Debra added.

'Oh, is he your boyfriend?'

'Well, sort of, but not serious.' Debra was evasive.

'I don't see anything wrong with that. If I liked somebody I would hold his hand, too.' Sandra shrugged her shoulder dismissing what, for her, was a perfectly friendly and harmless gesture.

'You better not, or do not let anyone see you,' Debra warned. 'The nuns have spies all over the island. But, I guess, you being white and all that, they probably wouldn't say anything to you. And, you being a big shot and all that.'

'How do you mean?' Sandra stopped walking to face Debra.

'You're new, so you don't know. If you're white or come from a rich family, they treat you differently. But if you're black and poor, they think your morals are low and have to be watched closely.'

'That is ridiculous!' Sandra raised her voice in protest. 'A person's character has nothing to do with the colour of their skin or whether they are rich or poor.'

'I agree with you. But it seems that's the way they look at it here.'

The girls walked in silence following the introduction of the colour question. Sandra was particularly concerned because it was becoming an important factor in her life. What with her father's attitude and now the nuns, she could only see racial conflicts in the future.

Debra's eyes were fixed on the young man in white chasing the cricket ball coming in their direction. 'Watch out, Sandra!' They stopped as the young cricketer picked up the ball, smiled to them and ran back to his game. 'It's the Grammar School!' Debra said excitedly. 'Can we watch for a while?'

Sandra smiled at the broad grin on Debra's face and wondered aloud, 'Does he play cricket?'

'Who, Daniel? Sometimes.' Her eyes roamed the field as she spoke.

'That's a nice name, Daniel,' Sandra repeated. 'Do you call him Danny?'

'Everybody calls him Danny,' she spoke his name with tenderness. 'But I call him Dan.'

'I can tell you like him a lot. He must be very handsome and full of fun.'

'Oh, he loves fun.' Debra was truly excited to talk about her boyfriend. 'He loves dancing and swimming. He goes to Rock-a-way every Sunday. That's where we meet mostly.'

'Where is that?'

'It's a beach just two miles down the coastal road going north. You passed it on your way to Roseau.'

'I must have, but it was dark. I'll have to go there one Sunday.' Sandra was enjoying Debra's happiness.

The cricket game was slow and dull, yet Debra showed more interest than was warranted. Suddenly, she was returning a hand wave to a player who was fielding at long leg. 'That's John Deshaut, a friend of Dan's,' she explained to Sandra. Soon, here and there, heads turned in their direction, including the umpires'.

'I think we'd better leave, Debie,' Sandra suggested. 'We seem to be distracting the players.'

'That's not our problem. They should mind their own business,' Debra objected. 'We are spectators, they are players.' As she spoke, a young man approached them from the side lines. 'Oh-oh! Don't look, but, here comes Mark, the lark.'

'Who's he?' Asked Sandra, looking straight ahead at the game.

'He's the banker's son. He's white, but he behaves as if he is black.' Debra replied in a muffled tone as she tried to stifle her laughter.

'Oh, Mark Radcliffe!' Sandra could not restrain her laughter. 'Mark, the lark!' She repeated with amusement. 'Why do you call him by that name?'

'You should hear how he talks. It's as if he sings all the time.' They both laughed.

But their laughter stopped abruptly when Mark greeted them. 'Hi Sandra, hi Debie. Wha's cookin'?' The music from Mark's voice brought giggles from the girls.

'Hi Mark,' Sandra answered. 'We're fine, thanks.' They tried desperately to restrain their laughter, but with little success.

'I see you girls are having a wonderful time. Want to share the joke?'

'No, sir!' Debra shook her head. 'That's for girls only,' she said between giggles. 'Besides, you should be in the pavilion. The master in charge might just report you to the head for roaming about when you should be with your team.'

'They won't need me anymore. I've batted already.'

'How much did you score?' Sandra asked.

'I layed me an egg. Quack! Quack!' He imitated the crying sound of a duck, then stooped to demonstrate the laying of an egg.

Debra turned to Sandra and said with utter seriousness, 'Well, birds lay eggs, don't they?' She meant "larks".

The two girls folded in ecstatic laughter, to Mark's surprise. All eyes turned in the direction of what was indeed a disturbance of the usual, peaceful atmosphere in the Botanic Gardens.

'Radcliffe!' The stern command from the pavilion was heard distinctly across the field.

'Sir!' Mark answered with equal gusto, then said goodbye to the girls and sprinted toward the pavilion.

Sandra and Debra regained their composure while the game resumed. Each crack of the bat against the ball echoed beneath the towering trees. Fielders darted about to retrieve the ball while the two batsmen dashed from crease to crease. The excitement waned.

Sandra looked at her watch. 'I must go now, Debie.' She stood up.

'I'll go through the gate with you, and we'll see tomorrow, okay?'

'Okay.' Sandra was pleased to have made another friend. 'I hope you will be able to come and visit me some time, Debie.'

'Sure. I live just down the road on the other side of the Gardens, near the Windsor Park.' Debra pointed in the direction of her neighbourhood. 'We could meet in the Gardens to revise for exams.'

'That would be nice,' Sandra agreed. 'I like the quietness there. The air is clean and the fresh smell of the flowers very inviting.'

'That's a deal, then. See you tomorrow.'

CHAPTER NINE

THE FOLLOWING weeks passed by with relative calm. Knowles Gardens was slowly regaining its popularity among the white community. The illness of Henry Knowles had brought a halt to the many social gatherings, tea parties for charity and the like. The circle of family friends, too, was expanding and so Betty, consumed with the desire to entertain as they were entertained, was busy redecorating the family home.

Bruce, too, was making every effort to get to know the white community, and consequently spent a good deal of time at the Red Rose. The Club was a legacy of the colonial masters which retained its white-only membership. Bruce felt very much at home there, particularly when he met someone who shared his prejudicial views in James Compton, heir to the Rosenhall Estate.

So, how are you coping with Barry?' James looked at Bruce with a quizzical grin.

'You mean Barry Manners, one of my field supervisors?' Bruce knew no other.

'That's the bastard!' James muttered over his glass of rum and ice.

'He hasn't given me any trouble. Why?'

James Compton smiled sadly, shaking his head regretfully. 'You know, your uncle Henry did a great disservice to the white community when he hired that bastard. My family and I have not spoken to Henry since. But you are different. You are like me. You let the black people know their place. But not Henry. He believed in the equality of man, black, white or yellow. But things will be different now, with you in command.'

'What did Barry do?' Bruce was anxious for more.

James smiled, grunted a laugh, then took a gulp of rum. He looked at Bruce with thoughtful eyes. 'Of course, you would not know. That was three years ago when the labourers revolted on all estates throughout the island. Barry was the headman on our estate, well paid and respected. In spite of that he led the revolt at Rosenhall. We would not give in to their demands, and they all left.'

'So what happened?'

'Well, strangely enough, the black people stuck together against us and we couldn't recruit another labourer for the estate for a long time.' James finished his drink and called for another.

'And my uncle went ahead and hired Barry?' Bruce finished the story for James. 'That's treachery!' he concluded, becoming entrapped in the web of bitterness that James Compton was weaving.

'That's exactly what the white community called Henry, a traitor to his race, the Judas of the white community!'

The icy countenance which seized the tanned face of James Compton matched the hardened jaws and narrowed eyelids of Bruce Knowles. Bruce was hurting inside, He had admired his uncle Henry as a boy. He was proud, too, of the excellent reputation his uncle had built in the community. How could he be regarded as a traitor by his people? Would he inherit this name, too, if Barry Manners stayed on at Riversdale?

'We could not understand your uncle's logic in employing two union men at Riversdale. The union was the enemy determined to destroy our livelihood. They say Henry employed Eugene to prevent an uprising at Riversdale and later, he took on Barry to demonstrate the good faith of white plantation owners.'

'What good faith? Bruce blurted out. 'The bastard destroys your brother's property and you thank him by giving him a job!'

'That's exactly how we felt, Bruce. The last laugh was on us. We were made to look like the villains, and I'm sorry, we have not been able to forgive your uncle to this day.'

'I can't blame you, James. I would have felt the same way,' Bruce empathised. 'Should we wonder, then, why Riversdale did not suffer the same fate as other plantations? Or why the workers there are not yet unionised?'

'Bruce,' James smiled, 'it takes only one poll to get unionised. If the situation warrants it, Riversdale could be unionised overnight. In this country, you don't need to belong to a union to operate under their rules. Eugene and Barry will ensure that wages and conditions of work are comparable for all unionised workers. Your uncle placed himself in a situation where he could not easily refuse workers' demands, union or no union.'

'Well,' Bruce raised his glass and gulped a mouthful, 'the situation will be different now. I have already told them the way I will be running things from now on. I have made it clear that Riversdale is not a charitable organisation. That I will not tolerate idleness or rudeness of any sort. That those who do not come up to my expectations will have to go!'

'And what was their reaction?'

Bruce did not reply immediately. He could not tell James that the workers walked out on him without him taking any punitive action against them. That would be a sign of weakness. 'They didn't like what I had to say, but realized I had the right to say it.' Bruce repeated the counselling that Eugene gave the workers.

'Good,' James congratulated him. 'You seem to have them under control. Three years ago, a threat like that would have resulted in public outcry. It would have been labelled worker harassment by the union, a complaint would have been lodged with the Labour Commissioner, and there would have been an investigation followed by a letter of reprimand.' James laughed heartily. 'No teeth at all, no teeth!'

'Let them go ahead,' Bruce smiled. 'The right to dismiss cannot be taken away from the employer in a free country. As long as there is just cause, no one can challenge my right to fire any of my workers.'

[85]

'I agree, Bruce. But you try to get rid of, say Barry, even with legitimate cause, and you will have the entire black community against you.'

Bruce Knowles sipped some rum punch and smiled. 'Let me say, James, it is my intention, when the opportunity arises, to rid myself and Riversdale of this blemish, Barry Manners. Between you and me, life for Barry won't be comfortable at Riversdale. Very soon I'll put a plan into action which will so frustrate him that he will resign of his own accord.'

James Compton smiled at Bruce, puzzled, but elated. At last, he thought, revenge for Rosenhall was on its way. Nothing would delight him more than to see Barry Manners thrown out of Riversdale, never to be employed again by white plantation owners. 'The day Barry Manners is struck off the pay roll of Riversdale Plantation, Bruce, you will become a hero among us. You will have rectified a wrong done by your uncle, and the solidarity of the white community would be restored.'

'You leave it to me, James.' A feeling of power rose within Bruce Knowles. 'I did not return to these backwoods of the Caribbean to go to bed with their women or drink rum with their men!'

With this declaration James Compton raised his glass and toasted, 'To white solidarity!'

Their glasses touched, and they drank.

Sandra and Debra had become very close friends. They met regularly at the Botanic Gardens to study for the Senior Cambridge examinations. It was at one of these sessions that Sandra had met Debra's boyfriend, Daniel Phillips. He was their topic of conversation one Saturday afternoon while strolling the experimental section of the Gardens.

'He wants to be a doctor, but he will have to win a scholarship because his family cannot afford tuition fees.' Debra revealed.

'That's good, Debie. I hope he does because he is very gentle with people,' Sandra smiled, 'and, he is not shy at all.'

'That's true,' Debra agreed. 'You know, the first time we met, he nearly swept me off my feet.' Debra laughed at her expression.

[86]

'Really?' Sandra exclaimed. 'He must be a descendent of Rudolph Valentino!' Their youthful laughter echoed against the surrounding hills.

'Actually, it was at a school dance at the St Gerrard's Hall. He is such a terrific dancer! All the girls wanted to dance with him.'

'I guess you were jealous when they did,' Sandra teased.

'Not really, because I didn't know him well then. But I get really mad now when he talks to other girls.'

'Then you are really in love with him.'

'You bet I am.' Debra was soft spoken in revealing her innermost feelings. 'I don't know what I'd do if we broke up.'

Sandra listened with interest to the confessions of her friend, and wondered what it was like to be in love. 'You know, Debie, I have never been in love.'

'Really?' Debra did not conceal her surprise.

'I had a couple of infatuations, but relationships were just superficial.' Sandra recalled with some amusement. 'I suppose we had fun, but they never lasted.'

'I had these relationships, too. Everybody gets infatuated when they are young. I guess this is the way we learn to recognise real love later on.'

'What's it really like to be in love?' Sandra looked at her friend in anxious anticipation.

Debra smiled. For a moment she was at a loss for words. She could draw only from her limited experience. But how could she explain her innermost feelings to Sandra? Do all lovers experience love alike? 'It's hard to explain love to someone else. I can tell you how it makes me feel, but I am not sure everyone feels the same way. To know that someone like Dan cares for me and wants to share his joys and sorrows with me makes me feel important. I can face life with more confidence just knowing that Dan is there when I feel down. You understand?'

Sandra nodded. 'It's like the confidence and support you have from knowing that your parents are always there to help you when you need them.'

'Well, not really.' Debra shook her head slightly. 'That's different. With parents it's more like dependence. It's a different kind of love, which we take for granted. You are born with this relationship. Parental love is all mixed up with obedience and respect, with guidance and discipline.' Debra paused to think about the comparison before continuing. 'But, with Dan, there is more intimacy and freedom in our relationship. When he holds me in his arms, I feel like I am in a beautiful dream and want to stay there forever.' Again, she paused to smile at the memory. 'And, when he kisses me, it's as if we become one person. My body feels like it melts into his. It's so beautiful.'

Sandra was smiling pleasantly as Debra's eyes filled with tears of joy. 'It must be wonderful to be in love.'

'You bet it is, Sandra.'

The girls arrived at their favourite bench and opened their books to commence their revision. But Sandra could not concentrate on her work. She kept leafing through the pages aimlessly.

Debra observed Sandra's restlessness. 'Are you falling in love, Sandra?'

'Oh, no!' Sandra laughed. 'Why do you think so?'

'Well, seeing that you asked me what it's like, and seeing that you are so lost in your thoughts, I just wondered.'

Sandra smiled. 'Actually, I was thinking what it would be like when I do fall in love. I am hoping it would be like you.'

'There aren't many white boys your age on the island. Their parents ship them off to Barbados or England where the education is no better than ours,' Debra commented innocently. 'So your choice is limited.'

Sandra laughed at the obvious implication of Debra's remark. 'I think you are prejudiced, Debra?' She said jokingly.

'What?' Debra did not understand.

'Why do you think I must fall in love with a white boy and not a black, handsome, young man like Danny?' Sandra was direct.

'Would you?' Debra was surprised.

'Wouldn't you have fallen in love with Danny if he were white?'

'Well, er, I don't know. I never thought of that. In fact, if Danny were white he wouldn't want a black girlfriend, anyway.'

[88]

'And why not?' Sandra persisted. 'What has the colour of the skin got to do with love?'

'You don't understand, Sandra. White people stick with their kind.'

'And, I suppose, black people stick with their kind, too.' Sandra took hold of Debra's hand to emphasise the contrast between them.

'I don't mean it that way, Sandra.' Debra became visibly embarrassed. 'Friendship is casual, but love is deep and intimate.'

'I know, Debie. But, it appears you wouldn't like the idea of me falling in love with a young black man.' Sandra smiled.

'I didn't say that,' Debra shook her head vigorously. 'As a matter of fact, I would be so happy I wouldn't know what to say.'

'That's good, because if a young man like Danny should sweep me off my feet I think I would fall in love just like you.'

Debra smiled shyly at Sandra's declaration, but, from her silence she was ill at ease. She turned suddenly to Sandra and said, 'Look, Sandra, I hope you don't really think I'm prejudiced because of what I said a while ago.'

Sandra smiled at the look of concern on her friend's face. 'Of course you are prejudiced. We are all prejudiced in one way or another. We all have likes and dislikes, and discriminate in favour of our likes and against our dislikes. Some white people dislike black people and want nothing to do with them, and, in the same way, some black people want nothing to do with white people.'

Debra sat silently, giving Sandra her full attention. Sandra was making a lot of sense and Debra wanted to pursue the subject. 'Are you saying it is natural and all right to be prejudiced?'

'Of course, it is. To be prejudiced is to have preconceived beliefs and opinions about people and things. If we didn't, how could we go about making choices? Imagine going through life without having to choose?'

'That would be a dull and aimless existence,' Debra nodded her understanding.

'Sure, it would,' Sandra echoed, 'but, in making our choices we have to consider the consequences for others.'

[89]

'I see what you mean.' Debra was impressed with Sandra's reasoning. 'But how do you know all this?'

'Well, it was the subject of a discussion we had on race relations at my school in London,' Sandra explained. 'As more and more black students enrolled at my school, some white parents were getting concerned about the effect this was going to have on white children. So the Parent Teachers Association organised a panel discussion on the subject.'

'That was smart,' Debra observed.

'It was then that I realised why some white parents expressed such terrible views about multiracial schools. You see, as the panel explained, people do have preconceived ideas about races, and in particular, about black people, which influence their behaviour toward these races. But, these prejudices are not based on truth, but on myth. They are just handed down from generation to generation and people believe them without having any first-hand experience to support their beliefs.'

'I see.' Debra was attentive.

'The panel concluded that we must give multiracial schools a fair chance before we can pass judgement on them.'

'That's fair enough,' Debra agreed, 'and were they a success?'

'Well, from what I've seen, our racial background has nothing to do with our ability to learn or relate to other people. I found school more exciting with black students.'

'What about the white parents who were concerned? Were they convinced that these prejudices were unfounded?'

'I'm afraid not, Debie,' Sandra said regretfully. 'Some were so set in their beliefs that they were demanding a specific percentage of black student enrolment. But the authorities were opposed.'

A moment of silence followed as Debra and Sandra reflected on their discussion. Debra was smiling as she gazed at her black hands. 'So you think I am prejudiced, eh, Sandra?'

'Well, what do you think?' Sandra smiled.

'Maybe you are right. But, I will not let my prejudices interfere with our friendship. After all, we are people first, with flesh and blood,' Debra concluded.

'And a heart that can love, as well as hate, irrespective of the colour of our skin,' Sandra added. 'That is what I believe is really important about people, that we are all human beings.'

'You want to hear something, Sandra?' Debra looked at her friend seriously. 'I was never fond of white people because of what they did to my race. So, when they put you to share my desk, I was annoyed. But almost immediately, you made me feel comfortable and we became friends. You see, it's the individual that matters, not his race or colour or whatever.'

'Yes, that's the way I look at it, Debie. If we all accept that, then we wouldn't hurt each other the way we do. We cannot change people's prejudices, especially those that are deep-rooted, but I hate to see these prejudices used to hurt others needlessly.'

'I agree,' Debie added quietly.

CHAPTER TEN

'CAN YOU SWIM?' Mark Radcliffe raised his eyebrows expecting an affirmative answer.

'I think so.' Sandra continued to paddle her feet in the water as they sat at the edge of the swimming pool at Knowles Gardens. 'We had lessons at school in London and I passed the test.'

'But, you have never swam in the sea?' Mark wondered.

'No, but I suppose it would be the same, wouldn't it?'

'I guess so,' Mark was doubtful, 'except you must know how to master the waves. It's more fun in the sea. Would you like to go with me to Rock-a-way next Sunday?'

'Rock-a-way!' Sandra became excited. 'Sure, I'd love to. Let me ask my dad.'

Bruce and Betty were entertaining the Radcliffe family. Their laughter rose against the background rushing of the river, as Errol Radcliffe told of some hilarious encounters he had with politicians. 'They seem to think because they are members of Government their right to preferential treatment is sacrosanct. It is really pathetic how blatantly they abuse their political power for their selfish ends.

'When I explained to him that the value of Crown lands which he acquired was inadequate collateral for the amount of loan he was asking, and would need at least one surety in good standing, he replied, "Mr Radcliffe, don't you know who I am? I am a Minister of Government, elected by the people. The people have placed their trust in me. Why would you wish to question this trust?"'

[93]

'The barefaced scoundrel,' Bruce interjected.

'Well, I replied with all the diplomacy at my command, that I respected the trust the people placed in him and that I would also appreciate his respect for the trust the depositors have placed in me, as Bank Manager.'

Sandra had come to stand beside her father as the laughter erupted. It was Betty who noticed her. 'What do you want, San?'

'Sorry to bother you, dad, but may I go to the beach with Mark next Sunday?'

'Of course, you may, San,' Bruce replied, and continued to enjoy the laughter.

Betty watched her daughter jump into the pool with joy to join Mark who was creating quite a splash with the execution of each butterfly stroke. She smiled when Sandra emerged from beneath the water and grabbed Mark by the leg. 'Aren't they having fun?' Betty turned to Martha Radcliffe.

'That's the story of Mark's life,' Martha smiled conservatively. 'For him, life is a never-ending party. He is very popular in the community, always out, seldom studies.' She shook her head with regret.

'This is his final year at school,' Errol joined in. 'I am taking him into the bank in September where I can keep an eye on him. He is extremely clever in matters of finance.'

'Guess he takes after you, Errol,' Bruce flattered. 'It is good to have a son follow in your footsteps. I think that's why I am here. Gives a sense of continuity.'

Betty eyed Bruce and smiled shyly. The thought which crossed her mind was as old as their marriage. Bruce had wanted a son and she knew the disappointment he felt when Sandra was born. But she could have no more children. She could not realise his dream.

'I believe it's the same with daughters,' Martha submitted. 'More and more women are taking on leadership positions in their communities. Even here on the island, it took a woman to reorganise the failing Union Movement. We have a female Minister of Government who, one day, could easily become the Premier. Even in agriculture, Bruce, there are many women who

[94]

manage and own plantations. Who knows, Sandra may be inclined to follow the tradition, too.'

Bruce laughed heartily at the suggestion. 'A small plantation, yes; but, to manage Riversdale you need to be tough and rough if you must command respect and obedience from hard-drinking, cutlass-wielding men and women.'

'Women are too delicate for some occupations, I agree,' Errol added, 'but, with a good team of supervisors like you have in Eugene, Tom and Barry, a woman who is keen could hold the reins at Riversdale.'

The mention of Barry Manners by the most reputable banker on the island brought a sudden shock to Bruce. He was more surprised by the positive way in which Errol Radcliffe spoke of the man. 'Do you know Barry well?' Bruce's curiosity was aroused.

'Oh yes,' Errol replied without hesitation, 'very well, actually. An occupational hazard, if you like. A banker cannot help knowing his most active clients,' Errol smiled.

'Well, I'm surprised. He didn't strike me as a man of means.' Bruce was puzzled. He became even more confused by the laughter from Martha and Errol.

'I'm sorry, Bruce,' Errol apologised, 'I misled you by the way I referred to Barry. I was alluding to the regularity of his loan repayments.' He paused to regain his composure before continuing. 'It's a long story how I got to know Barry, but, I guess you will hear about it sooner or later. You must have heard about the labour problems plantation owners suffered a few years ago?'

'Yes, I do,' Bruce confirmed, 'and I know of the problems of Rosenhall in which Barry Manners featured prominently.'

'You do?' It was Errol's turn for surprises.

'I do. And, it bothers me that my uncle had the gall to employ Barry after what he did to Rosenhall and the Comptons.'

The silence was instant. Errol eyed Martha then turned to Bruce. 'What did you hear about Barry and Rosenhall?'

Bruce caught the eager, but perplexed eyes of his wife, Betty. What he was about to reveal was yet unknown to her. 'I understand Barry was the one who led the uprising at Rosenhall which brought down the estate. That he threatened the Comptons with violence and arson which led the family to seek and obtain police protection. And, in the face of this attack on a defenceless white family, uncle Henry employed Barry at Riversdale.'

All eyebrows were raised. Errol and Martha looked at each other sorrowfully.

Betty remained confused, but her sympathies were clearly with her husband whose look of indignation cried out for action. 'Really!' she exclaimed. 'How could uncle Henry do such a thing?'

'Beats me,' Bruce replied. 'Apparently, he was looked upon as a traitor by the white community here.'

'Now, hold on!' Errol raised his voice defensively. 'You've got it all wrong, Bruce. It's obvious you've been talking with James Compton himself. Am I right?'

'Yes, you are. I was told about it by the victim himself. Why?'

'I'm afraid, Bruce, it's you who became the victim of Compton's lies and deceit.' Errol was annoyed. 'Did he tell you he opposed the white farming community when they proposed a settlement with the workers?'

'No, he didn't.'

'Of course, he wouldn't. Did he tell you that he aroused the indignation of the farming community when he shot and killed two cattle which strayed onto Rosenhall from the nearby village, during the strike?'

'No.'

'And I guess he also failed to mention the fact that he refused to pay wages owed, unless the workers called off their strike.'

Bruce shook his head.

'Here are the true facts, Bruce,' Errol turned to face him squarely. 'As Union representative, Barry negotiated with James on behalf of the workers. No one should hold Barry responsible, personally, for the downfall of Rosenhall. Threats of arson came from the village in retaliation for the slaying of their cattle. And as for your uncle's generosity to Barry, you may as well know that Henry's decision to employ him was merely an arrangement worked out between them so that Barry could continue payments to our bank on a loan which Henry had backed.'

As these revelations were brought to light, the worried frowns on Betty's brow melted away. She exchanged smiles with Martha. Errol sipped rum punch while he gazed at the still perplexed look on Bruce's face.

'Don't look so worried, Bruce,' Errol tried to reassure him. 'No one in the white community has ever regarded your uncle as a traitor – except perhaps James Compton.'

'Then, why should he deliberately lie to me?' Bruce felt cheated. 'He must have realised that, sooner or later, I would know the true story.'

'I guess he is still seeking revenge against Barry for what happened to Rosenhall,' Errol suggested.

'And he is using you, dear, as an ally,' Betty joined in. 'Since Barry works for you now, you would hardly want to keep him considering what James claimed he did to Rosenhall and the Compton family.'

'Exactly,' Errol agreed.

Bruce pulled on his pipe as he listened to Betty and Errol confirm his own thoughts about James Compton. Why should James call his uncle a traitor? Did James know why his uncle employed Barry? Of course not. And why was James placing the full responsibility for the demise of Rosenhall on Barry?

'It seems to me,' Bruce did not remove his pipe as he spoke, 'there is a lot of animosity between Barry and James. I can't understand why James would still want to persecute Barry for something which happened three years ago.' He sucked on his pipe.

'In spite of his involvement with Rosenhall, Barry is much admired by the white community,' Errol revealed. Then, turning to his wife, he smiled and asked, 'I wonder if James is still upset over Emily?'

'Wouldn't surprise me in the least,' Martha whispered back.

'And who is Emily?' Betty's curiosity was quickly awakened.

'She's James's sister, now living in Barbados.' Martha paused to consider what she should say next. 'It's an old story, Betty, concerning her affair with Barry.'

'Barry was involved with James's sister?' Bruce jumped in.

Martha nodded. 'The relationship was so close that when Emily became pregnant, she was shipped to Barbados to avoid the scandal,' Martha concluded.

'Well, well!' Bruce muttered. 'So Barry stepped out of line and James didn't like it.'

'Not so,' Errol corrected. 'Emily was well known to be a flirtatious woman. In fact, she was a constant embarrassment to her family. She loved parties and drank heavily. She had liked Barry, but he despised her way of life. Her parents thought he would bring some stability and maybe respectability to her life, and encouraged the relationship, much to the chagrin of their son James.' Errol took a long sip from his drink and sighed deeply.

'You see, James disliked black people,' Martha continued the story. 'When she became pregnant, Barry offered to marry her, but it appears, unknown to him, she had been seeing another man, a white Venezuelan. She could not make up her mind, even though encouraged by her parents. But James told Barry about the other lover with the obvious intention of preventing the marriage. Naturally, Barry became doubtful of his paternity, and would no longer consider marriage. In the meantime, the Venezuelan left the island and Emily was alone.'

'Her parents, surprisingly, understood Barry's feelings, and Emily accepted their offer to support her and her child in Barbados.' Errol completed the story.

There was silence following the revelations. Bruce reclined on his chair with eyes closed and pipe perched comfortably in his mouth. Martha and Betty took the opportunity to join Mark and Sandra by the pool.

Still with eyes closed, Bruce removed his pipe and commented, 'Well, Errol, times have changed, indeed. Who would have thought black and white would one day consider marriage. The very thought of sexual intimacy turns my stomach. But marriage! How could the Comptons face the white community?'

'You answered yourself, Bruce,' Errol replied. 'The island you left twenty-five years ago no longer exists. You see, it is inevitable when people of different races live together that, through the magic of time, they eventually shed their racial cloaks and reveal themselves as human beings, which we all are. Whether white or black, we all have feelings and desires which only other human beings can share and satisfy. Love, friendship, respect, caring, all these transcend the barriers of race, colour or any other cultural difference.' Errol stopped to smile in appreciation of his own words, then added, 'And rightly so.'

'So, are you saying you would agree if Mark were to marry a black girl?' Bruce sat up, gazed at Errol with raised eyebrows.

Errol chuckled. 'This is, of course, hypothetical. However, it would not be a question of my agreeing or not. I hope I would be mature enough to base my feelings on the genuineness of their love for each other.'

'Interesting,' Bruce observed, 'very interesting.'

'And what about your Sandra? How would you feel if she proposed to marry a black man? Would you approve?'

Bruce's response was immediate and emphatic. 'Never!' He shook his head vigorously. 'It would be the final betrayal!'

Errol was surprised at Bruce's sudden change of countenance. His placid forehead was now an ocean of ripples. He saw his eyes narrow and lips purse when he removed his pipe. He saw Bruce sit up, gaze intently at his glass of rum punch and repeat, 'Never!'

CHAPTER ELEVEN

ROCK-A-WAY beach was buzzing with activity. Steel band music rang out above the rhythmic tumbling of the waves, while heads and bodies moved hypnotically to the beat. It was a typical Sunday afternoon. The blazing sun was generous in its brilliance, lighting up the Caribbean Sea in myriads of glistening sparkles as the ripples danced to the beat of nature.

Sandra smiled, admiringly, at the fearless display of Debra's torso movement, as she enjoyed the music. 'You remind me of Simone, a friend in England. She loved dancing to calypso music.'

'Can you?' Debra asked.

'I've never tried.'

'But you like dancing, I hope?' Debra expected the affirmative.

'I guess I do. I've been to some parties in London, but not to a real dance,' Sandra confessed.

Dancing is such a popular form of entertainment in the Caribbean that if you did not take part you were either a member of some religious sect which regarded it as sinful, or you were prohibited by your parents. 'Don't your parents approve of dancing?' Debra assumed.

'They love it,' Sandra replied. 'They went ballroom dancing very often. But I have not really had the opportunity to go. I guess one should have an escort and an invitation.'

Sandra's remark provoked an immediate chuckle from her friend. 'That's old fashioned, Sandra.' Debra smiled. 'Women are liberated in the Caribbean. Because we live in such small, close-knit communities, we chaperone one another. We look out for one another.'

'I noticed that,' Sandra nodded. 'It seems everybody knows everybody else. Everyone smiles to you even though they are strangers.'

'But that has its disadvantages as well,' Debra added sombrely.

'How do you mean?'

'Well, in the sense that you do not live much of a private life. 'People tend to mind your business, draw wrong conclusion from what they see, and generally gossip about you.'

'Why should this be a disadvantage if you live a clean, moral life with nothing to hide?' Sandra observed.

'Because these gossipers twist the truth into malicious falsehood, and the moral into the immoral, just for the fun of it!' Debra's tone was somewhat harsh.

'That's terrible,' Sandra agreed. 'One would think, though, people would recognise the truth when they hear it.'

'Ha ha!' Debra laughed. 'Well, don't be surprised, San, if Mother Rosa talks to you tomorrow about your unbecoming behaviour at Rock-a-way beach today,' she warned, and continued her laughter.

'What behaviour?'

'For instance,' Debra continued, 'how you wore a skimpy bathing suit, how you were surrounded by all the boys, and, perhaps, your tantalising display to attract them.'

They were both laughing so ecstatically at Debra's example of distorting the truth that they did not hear Mark, Daniel and John Deshaut approaching from behind.

'Want to share the joke?' Daniel's voice brought an instant halt to the laughter.

They turned abruptly to stare at the young men. Then, Debra turned to Sandra. 'See what I mean by attracting the boys?' They both resumed their laughing, but Sandra was more restrained in the presence of the stranger, John Deshaut.

'So, you all tryin' to attrac' de boys an' dem?' Mark joked colloquially. 'Well, Sandra, meet one of de boys.'

'Hi, Sandra.' John's voice sang his greeting, while his eyes and glimmering teeth showed a happy-to-meet-you smile.

'Hi,' was all that Sandra could say because she felt a lump in her throat when their hands joined. She then turned to Debra and let out a girlish giggle.

'But wait! What you playin' shy so, Sandra,' Mark joked once more. 'Is so you want to attrac' de boys an' dem?'

The laughter which followed was uncontrollable. Mark ended up rolling on the sand, tears of joy filled Sandra's and Debra's eyes, while John and Daniel looked on, both grinning from ear to ear.

John was the first to speak following this hilarity. 'So, how do you like us crazy people, Sandra?'

'Very much, so far,' Sandra smiled. 'You people are so full of fun, it's refreshing.'

'I hope you, too, will have some fun while you are here,' John encouraged.

'I intend to, and I am starting today.'

'Then, I expect to see you at the school dance on August Monday?' John invited.

'This is what I was going to tell you about, San,' Debra joined in. 'That's why I asked you if you liked dancing.'

'I would like to go, of course,' Sandra was eager. 'But I'll have to get dad's permission.'

'If he let you come to Rock-a-way, then he should let you attend our dance, which is organized by our school,' John reasoned.

'You don't know my father,' Sandra shook her head doubtfully. 'But if Mark is going, he could be my escort. Maybe dad would let me go.' She turned to Mark for his response.

'It would be my pleasure to escort you to the ball, Princess Sandra.' Mark stood up, then courtesied with a grand sweep of his right hand and let himself sprawl face downward, on the sand.

'You are such a clown,' Debra remarked as their laughter subsided. 'I guess that's why you are so popular.'

'No Debs, it's my charm,' Mark replied. 'You see, I am to the ladies what nectar is to the honey bee. I am irresistible.' Then dropping to his knees, Mark puckered his lips and leaned toward Debra saying, 'Try me, you'll like me.'

With this new eruption of laughter, Debra reacted by throwing handfuls of sand at Mark, who scampered to the safety of the warm sea, chased by Debra, Daniel, Sandra and finally John.

The sea foamed as bathers were engaging in their various activities. Two young ladies, wearing scanty bikinis and standing on the shoulders of two muscular men, were battling to dethrone each other. The men were jostling from side to side to maintain their balance. The splash which followed when one lady succumbed, left Sandra shouting in fits of laughter.

A group of four boys were freestyling, encouraged by the frantic cheers of onlookers. Another group were playing catchers with a red sponge ball. Several youngsters were perched on inflated car inner tubes, floating aimlessly on the bobbing waves.

But Sandra's attention settled on the lovers in warm embrace, admiring each other. He kissed her brow, then her nose, and finally her lips. Sandra smiled, then turned to face her own group. The admiring gaze of John Deshaut caught her eyes. She lowered her head slightly, feeling awkward by the unexpected encounter.

'Is this your first time on the beach?' John asked.

'Yes,' Sandra nodded.

'I could tell by the way you were so absorbed in everything.' John drew closer to Sandra.

'It is so different from England,' Sandra observed. 'Everything is so spontaneous, so casual, it makes you feel like joining in.'

'Yes, that's true. It's one of the best ways to relax, and it's all free from mother nature.' He smiled.

Sandra smiled, feeling more at ease in his presence. 'So why do you people leave all this warmth and fun for cold places like England and Canada?' she asked.

John laughed. 'You're not the first person to ask that, and it is always asked in connection with the weather. Don't you have nice, warm summers in England?'

'Sometimes, but you have it all year round. No winters, no snow, no winter coats, no heavy boots.'

'We have heavy rains and hurricanes which are more devastat ing than your winters,' John countered.

'Maybe,' Sandra granted, 'but would you exchange your hurricanes, which don't happen too often, for our regular winters in England?'

'Well, yes,' John smiled. 'But only if I had someone like you to keep me warm.'

Sandra laughed briefly and nervously, for she was neither prepared for nor knew how to respond to such romantic advances. She noticed the glimmer and sincerity in John's eyes, even though he had said it in jest. Instinctively, she scooped some water in her cupped hands and splashed his face in an effort to hide her surfacing blush.

John spun around to avoid the impact, and laughed while he continued to answer the question. 'To be honest, I really don't know why we emigrate nowadays. In the past, it would be to pursue educational advancement, but this is no longer a valid reason, since we have more opportunity in the Caribbean today. Some say life is better in the developed countries, plenty jobs, good salaries, spacious homes, and more opportunities generally.'

'I suppose those are good enough reasons for anyone seeking material gain,' Sandra said, thoughtfully. 'But in my opinion, a better life should not be measured in pounds, shillings and pence.'

'This is how I feel, too,' John agreed. 'But, you know what they say, "the grass is always greener on the other side of the fence".' They laughed.

Their eyes met following their laughter. It was for an instant, but Sandra's heart moved within. She felt awkward, so hastened to say, 'I would prefer to live here than in England. As a matter of fact my roots are right here in Dominica.'

'Your parents are Dominicans?' John asked with surprise.

'Only my father. His parents were English but he was born here.'

Sandra and John spoke of many things as they stood soaking-in the warm, soothing waters of the Caribbean Sea. They spoke of their aspirations, about life in England as compared with

[105]

Dominica. After some time, John began smiling as he gazed at Sandra.

Sandra stopped what she was saying and smiled back, asking, 'What are you smiling at?'

'Do you realise we've only just met, and here we are, sharing our personal ambitions. It is as if we knew each other long before.'

'Yes, that's true,' Sandra faced him squarely. 'I don't usually talk to strangers that openly, but somehow you're different.'

'I know why,' John said softly.

'Why?'

'Because, I believe we complement each other,' John advanced his theory.

'What do you mean?' Sandra became curious.

'Well let's put it this way,' John explained. 'Look at the blackboard and easel at school. Without the easel the blackboard cannot stand, and without the blackboard the easel is useless. They support each other.'

'What you are saying is that together you and I help each other to be, eh, what's the word?' Sandra could not find the appropriate word.

'Whole?' John suggested.

'Something like that,' she nodded. 'We are like twins.' Sandra smiled, then said, jokingly, 'Black and white twins!' She laughed. 'That's funny, don't you think?'

John smiled at Sandra's imagination. He saw the oddity of the comparison, but was not particularly amused. 'Let's just say, you and I can become very close friends because we are compatible, Sandra.'

Sandra was silent now. It was the gentle seriousness in John's voice which struck a chord deep in her being. She felt he was offering more than friendship, and she could not say no. 'Sure, we can be friends. I would like that.' Sandra heard the words deep within her. Could this be the start of something wonderful?

John smiled. 'You have made me happy, Sandra. Maybe, someday you might welcome me into your heart as well.'

Sandra could no longer restrain her blushing. She felt her

[106]

heart flutter in agreement with John's wishes. She smiled but could not speak. Yet, she had a burning desire to say she would, not in words, but in action. So, in utterly puerile reaction, she splashed some more water into his face, laughing heartily. He did not resist, but fought back with splashes of his own, causing her to swim away from him to rejoin the group.

CHAPTER TWELVE

MABLE STOOD by the window staring at Betty Knowles who lay sunbathing by the swimming pool. In the past this would have brought joy to her heart, but now Mable was more concerned about the bottle of rum punch beside her. Betty had taken to drinking all hours of the day, and it was apparent that she had become addicted to the drink. Bruce was no help to Betty since he, too, found the drink 'rather refreshing and harmless', to quote his expression. But Mable saw what disastrous effect it was having on Betty, and decided she was no longer concocting the beverage.

Mable did not hear Sandra walk in from school. She literally jumped when Sandra shouted out her usual hearty greetings. Mable held her hands to her chest, panting, 'Chil', you frighten me. Lord!' She breathed deeply. 'I don' hear you come in, an' my min' far away.'

'Sorry, Mabes,' Sandra apologised, 'I didn't mean to frighten you.' She gave Mable a warm hug. 'Where's mom?'

'She by de pool, drinkin' again,' Mable replied sadly.

Sandra looked out of the window to see her mother gulping a mouthful of punch. She shook her head hopelessly, turned to Mable and said, 'I thought you weren't making any more rum punch, Mabes.'

'Dis is de las' bottle,' Mable explained. 'She take it before I able to hide it. But I not makin' no more, Miss Sandra. Dis is de las' one, for sure!'

As Mable and Sandra were talking, Betty reached for the bottle to refill her glass and carelessly knocked it over. 'Damn!'

She exclaimed in disgust, grabbing at the rolling bottle but could not stop it from entering the pool. She sat up in frustration and shouted, 'Mable!'

'Yes, Miss Betty,' Mable hurried to the poolside. She had seen the accident and guessed Betty would be asking for another bottle of punch. 'Look me, mam,' she said.

'Would you fetch me another bottle of punch, please. The other one fell into the pool.' Betty sounded apologetic.

'It finish, Miss Betty. We don' have no more.' Mable said. 'We don' have no white rum, no spice, an' no limes. De only fing we have is bitters.'

'Well, hurry up and make some more,' Betty urged.

'Yes, mam,' Mable replied dryly, leaving Betty to continue her tanning in the sun.

Sandra observed the scene from the window and wondered what could be done to discourage her mother from this excessive indulgence. She walked to her bedroom feeling very concerned that her mother might become an embarrassment to the family if her dependency went unchecked. What would her friend Debie think if she knew her mother was an alcoholic, she thought. And, what about John Deshaut, her new-found boyfriend? What would he think? These thoughts occupied Sandra's mind while she was changing into casual wear. When she stepped out of her room, she saw her mother staggering in the living room.

'Hi, San,' her mother greeted, 'how was school today?'

'Okay.' Sandra was more interested in her mother's drunken state. 'Mom, are you all right?'

'Sure, I'm all right,' Betty replied, smiling as she approached her daughter. 'I just had a little too much to drink, that's all.' Betty repeated the usual explanation for her drunkenness.

'Mom, please stop that drinking,' Sandra pleaded. 'You are going to get very ill from that rum punch, one day.'

Betty exploded defensively. 'Oh, shut up, Sandra! You are beginning to sound like your father.' She walked away from her daughter and sat heavily on the settee. 'You're both always preaching to me about my drinking. This is becoming ridiculous now. I drink in the privacy of my home. I am not an alcoholic. So what's all the fuss about?'

Sandra had no answer. But she looked at Mable approaching from the kitchen and shrugged her shoulders helplessly. Mable responded by opening her big eyes wide, like a frightened child.

'Your tea ready, Miss Sandra.' Mable brought in a tray and placed it on the coffee table. 'You want tea, too, mam?' She asked Betty.

'No thanks, Mable.' Betty reclined on the settee. 'It's not like in London, San, is it?' Betty lamented. 'We would sit together and talk while we had tea. But these days we don't see dad. He is always busy at the estate or drinking with friends at the Red Rose. He hasn't much time for us, San.' Betty was almost in tears. 'I guess that's why I drink so much.'

Sandra had not touched her tea; her heart went out to her mother, who was hurting. She left the tray to sit next to her mother, placing her arms around her. 'Mom, why don't you tell dad how you feel about this? If he knew you felt this way, I'm sure he would try to be home earlier and more often.'

'I told him already, but he said he was too occupied with labour problems at Riversdale. He was right. The workers are on strike.'

'I know,' Sandra said. 'Some students are saying that dad is a racist. That he was treating the labourers like slaves, so they went on strike. They say they are going to burn the estate if dad does not change the way he is treating them.'

Betty was alert once more. 'You heard that at school?'

'Today,' Sandra confirmed. 'My friend Debie told me she heard some girls talking about the strike, and that one said the next step was "de feu", which means fire.'

'I wish Bruce would let me know what is happening.' Betty was concerned after hearing these stories. 'We must take these rumours seriously. His life could be in danger.' She began pacing the floor, thirsting for a drink. 'He is so stubborn, he never listens to me these days.' She shook her head. 'I don't know, San, maybe we made a mistake coming.'

[111]

The thought of returning to London was not well received by Sandra. Her life was becoming very interesting. She was a young woman of importance, in a family of very high standing on the island. Her circle of friends was expanding and most of all she found herself falling in love for the first time. This new experience was the most exciting of all, and would not want to end it. 'Mom, why don't we talk to daddy together.' Sandra realised the situation was more serious than it appeared. 'Maybe he needs to remember why we came here. I think he should discuss his problems with us as he used to in England. What do you think?'

Betty was sitting once more. Her thoughts were in London remembering the less opulent but nonetheless comfortable life she had been used to. She thought of her friends in London and all the good wishes she received at the farewell party. Then her smile faded when Bruce's attitude to blacks came to mind. 'Do you think your father is a racist?'

'Maybe he is, mom,' Sandra said flatly. 'You remember what you told me at London Airport?'

'I warned him about his attitude to these people,' Betty grieved. 'I knew this would happen one day, all because of a childhood incident.'

'What childhood incident?' Sandra inquired.

'I'll tell you some day.'

'Why not now?' Sandra was anxious.

'Maybe soon, San,' Betty nodded. 'The way things are going, I believe it is becoming necessary to tell you so you can understand the root of your father's problem.'

'But I don't understand how dad could hate blacks and be so fond of Mable who is black.' Sandra was puzzled.

'Mable grew up with your father in this house, San. They were childhood friends who were separated by time. Your father always liked Mable, and the strength of their friendship has a lot to do with the childhood incident we will talk about.' She smiled, then laughed. 'I wonder if she has heard anything about dad from the local people?'

'Shall we ask her, mom?' Sandra became excited.

'Good idea. Mable,' Betty called, 'could we see you a minute?'

[112]

'Yes, mam,' Mable answered from the kitchen, 'I comin' jus' now.'

Mable entered quickly, wiping her hands on her apron. 'Look me, mam.'

'Mable, tell me the truth,' Betty began frankly. 'Have you been hearing bad news about Mr Bruce in town?'

'Don' believe noffing you hear dem say, mam,' Mable was protective of Bruce. 'Dese Dominicans always bad talkin' white people. Dose people don' have noffing to do, so dey on'y spen'in' deir time talkin' about people.'

'What are they saying about Mr Bruce?' Betty prompted.

'Some people say Brucie don' like us black. So, I a'ks dem if I white? So dey say I am a slave. You an' Mr Brucie workin' me like a donkey. So, I tell dem is better to work like a donkey dan to sit by de roadside bad talkin' people.'

'I'm sorry, Mabes,' Betty apologised. 'Why didn't you tell us about this before?'

'Because is not true, mam,' Mable said flatly. 'You an' Brucie treat me good, jus' like Mr Charles an' Mr Henry.'

'Is that all you've heard?' Betty probed further.

'I hear dem say fings bad on de estate wif de labourers, an' is Mr Bruce fault. Dey even say somebody goin' to burn dong de place for dat.'

Betty and Sandra remained silent after this confirmation of the rumours. Betty was sober now and was craving a drink. She licked her dry lips. 'Would you get me a beer, please, Mable? I'm thirsty.'

'Your tea ready, yes, mam?' Mable suggested.

Betty raised her head to see both Sandra and Mable looking at her with sorrowful eyes. Their message was clearly against the beer and in favour of the tea. 'All right, I'll have the tea now,' she obliged.

Mable did not hide her joy at Betty's preference. 'Yes, mam,' she said, and turned to leave, but stopped suddenly. 'Not to worry, Miss Betty,' she reassured, 'nobody not goin' to burn dong no garden. If dey burn dong de garden, how dey goin' an' feed deir famaly?' With these words, she hurried to the kitchen.

*   *   *

The sun was set and the evening breeze bathed the river valley with refreshing coolness. Roosters everywhere were bidding farewell to the day with a continuous chorus of cock-a-doodle-doos, while the hens were flapping their wings nervously as they settled in their tree-beds for the night.

Betty was once more at the poolside drinking beer. Sandra was doing her homework in the study, while Mable was busy preparing supper. Janet, the assistant to Mable, was gathering the day's washing when she observed Betty gulping down her drink directly from the bottle although there was a glass beside her. Janet smiled and continued her chores. Then she observed Betty attempt to stand, but fall back into her chair. Janet dropped the dried clothes and rushed to Betty's side. 'You awright, mam?'

'Yes,' Betty began to laugh, 'I j–just had a little t–too much t–to drink,' she stammered drunkenly. 'C–could you help me up p–please?'

'Yes, mam.' Janet took Betty's arm and helped her to her feet. She watched Betty stagger to the door, hold it, then enter the corridor leading to the living room. Janet shook her head and muttered, 'Bon dieu, I don' want to be rich, non. I happy how I am, oui, papa.' She shook her head once more, and turned to return to her chores when, suddenly, there was a heavy crash inside the house. She ran in, almost colliding with Sandra who had also responded to the noise. They both met Mable rushing to Betty's assistance.

Betty was laughing at her demise, unmindful of the depth of concern which was being shown for her wellbeing. 'Mom!' Sandra shouted. 'Are you all right?'

'Yes, dear,' Betty replied as she was helped to her feet.

'What happened?' Sandra asked.

'She drunk, Miss Sandra,' Janet whispered.

'I am not d–drunk!' Betty objected feebly. 'I j–just had a little t–too much t–to drink, that's all,' she stuttered.

'C'mon, mom,' Sandra held her mother lovingly by the waist, 'let me put you to bed; you look very tired.'

'Yes, dear,' Betty accepted willingly, 'I am v–very t–tired.'

Sandra's eyes filled with tears as she helped her mother to the safety of her room. She could not understand why her mother had taken to drinking so heavily. She wondered whether her father was aware of the seriousness of her mother's drinking. If not, then it was time he knew. Betty was becoming an embarrassment in the eyes of the domestic workers, and, sooner or later, it would be common knowledge in the community that she was an alcoholic. Sandra's eyes closed as she considered these thoughts painfully, and a teardrop rolled down her left cheek. She looked at her mother, asleep now, and said, 'Mom, I cannot let you destroy yourself like this. This is not why we came to Dominica.'

Sandra joined Mable who was preparing the table for dinner. Their sad eyes met, but no words were spoken. Sandra sat on the couch in the living room, lost in thought, while Mable continued setting the table. They both heard the jeep drive into the garage and looked in the direction of the door through which Bruce always entered.

He walked in to greet two sullen faces. He stopped, looking from one to the other. 'Good evening, Mabes.'

'Hello, Brucie,' Mable answered quietly.

'What's the matter, San? Had a bad day at school?'

'Dad, can I talk with you about mom?' Sandra begged.

'Why, what's the matter?' Bruce asked anxiously. 'Where is she?'

'Asleep. She's okay. But, there is something you should know about, before it gets worse.'

'What's that?'

'She was drunk, and she fell down in the living room.'

'What!' Bruce exclaimed and hurried to the bedroom, followed by Sandra. 'She didn't hurt herself, did she?'

'I don't think so. But I am worried she might become an alcoholic.' Sandra expressed her concern candidly.

'Don't be silly, Sandra,' Bruce reacted protectively, 'your mother is no alcoholic. She just can't hold her drinks. I've told her so repeatedly. You get drunk when you can't hold your drinks. But, you're an alcoholic when you can't do without a drink.'

[115]

'Well, I don't like seeing her drunk,' Sandra said painfully. 'People laugh and tease the drunkards on the streets of Roseau. I don't like to see her drunk, that's all.' Sandra was at the point of tears.

'Okay, I'll talk with her about it. I don't like it either,' Bruce agreed.

As they entered the bedroom, Betty stirred, yawned, and turned to her side. She groaned, holding her right knee.

'I think that's where she fell, on her right side,' Sandra remembered. 'She must have hurt it.'

'San,' Betty called, when she heard her daughter speak.

'Yes, mom.'

'My knee hurts.' She turned on her back and opened her eyes to see Bruce facing her. 'Bruce,' she cried, 'my right side hurts badly.'

'I better call Dr Korbinsky.' Bruce hurried to the telephone.

'Mom, don't you remember – you fell in the living room?'

'Did I?'

'You were drunk, mom,' Sandra said chastisingly.

Betty retorted in anger, sitting up painfully. 'I was not! How dare you say such a thing to me!'

Sandra quickly realised how embarrassing her mother must feel to be called drunk, and apologised immediately. 'I'm sorry, mom, but when you fell, you must have had too much to drink. That's why you can't remember it.' Sandra was more tactful.

'Maybe I did,' Betty accepted this explanation. 'I'll have to be more careful in future.'

Bruce returned to say that Henry Korbinsky was on his way. 'How are you feeling?' he asked his wife.

'Sandra was saying I had too much to drink and, well, I guess I lost my balance and fell,' Betty rationalised.

'From now on, I don't want you drinking alone in the house,' Bruce declared. 'You obviously have no control over the amount you take. I don't want you becoming dependent upon it.'

'What are you trying to say, Bruce?' Betty reacted defensively. 'That I am an alcoholic?'

[116]

'I am saying, let's be sure you don't become one.'

'That's absurd!' Betty said defiantly. 'I am alone all day, with nothing to do, so I take the occasional drink to pass the time, that's all. You have your work, Sandra is at school, Mable looks after the house. What am I to do?'

'There are a few voluntary organisations you can get involved with in the community,' Bruce explained. 'Why don't you talk with Martha Radcliffe?'

Betty shook her head and smiled. 'I just want to be with you and San the way we used to in London. I miss that a lot, love.' Betty took his hand. Sandra smiled.

'You had a full-time job, too, in London, don't forget,' Bruce reminded. 'You need to make more constructive use of your time. That's why I am suggesting voluntary work.'

'Would you mind if I joined one of the black voluntary organisations?' Betty looked at Bruce intently.

'There aren't any,' Bruce said flatly. 'They wouldn't know how to begin.'

'Well, I've attended two meetings of Martha's group and I am convinced their only purpose is getting together to drink tea and gossip,' Betty revealed. 'They solicit funds when necessary, and do nothing else. I can't be involved in something so unproductive. There are so many poor children running around the streets of Roseau, whose parents think they are at school, or who probably have no parents. Why can't something be done about that? Have you seen the undernourished kids at the Roseau Clinic? What are the rich people of Dominica doing to help them?'

'You are being ridiculous, Betty,' Bruce remarked. 'Why do you think there are governments? Why do we pay taxes? Why are black parents not shouldering their own responsibilities?' Bruce raised both hands for emphasis, then he said, 'But why are we discussing black people's problems, anyway?'

'Because that's where I would like to do some voluntary work,' Betty repeated. 'What is the justification for raising funds for the convent's favourite charity? Don't the sick children need medicines? They are always in short supply. Why can't funds be raised

[117]

for this purpose? The Government and taxes cannot do it all, not even in England. That is where I feel I can be more productive with my time.'

'I have to admit, you do have a point,' Bruce said. 'This is a poor country. When I pass through the villages to the estate, I see poverty everywhere. But, the people are happy in their poverty.'

'No, they are not,' Sandra finally joined in the conversation. 'They are satisfied with what they have because they don't know better, dad. In our last discussion group at school, the teacher said the whole point of education is to improve standards of living. If we don't strive for a better life we remain blissfully ignorant.'

Bruce smiled at his daughter's presentation. 'You are getting wiser everyday,' he said, 'but, you will find to be blissfully ignorant is the same as being happy in one's poverty.' He smiled when Sandra narrowed her eyelids in thought before she shook her head in disagreement.

'No, dad, on the contrary, ignorance breeds poverty, for if they knew how to improve their lot, they would not sit idly and accept poverty.'

'I guess that's why your workers are on strike,' Betty said casually. 'They are not prepared to let anything or anyone take away their happiness. They cherish their new standards enough to defend it.'

'What are you talking about?' Bruce reacted angrily. 'What do you know about this strike, Betty?'

'Nothing, really,' she replied calmly. 'I was only using it as an example to explain how people will stand up and agitate for what they believe is right, which is what you are saying, aren't you, San?'

Sandra nodded.

Bruce was at a loss for words, for Betty's analogy could not be denied. She was not passing judgement on the strike, as Bruce had assumed. 'Oh,' was all he offered in response.

'So what about the strike, dad?' Sandra seized the opportunity to introduce the subject. 'What are you going to do about it?'

'Let's not talk about that, please,' Bruce dismissed the subject. 'I have had a bellyful of it today from Clifford.'

'Me, too, at school,' Sandra added. 'They are calling you racist dad, and some are saying the workers are going to burn the estate if you don't change your attitude.'

'Is that so?' Bruce asked defiantly.

'I am very worried, love,' Betty pleaded. 'We are newcomers in this country. I don't want Sandra exposed to this kind of treatment at school. As for me, I am like a prisoner here. Who knows what can happen? We were a family in England, but now, we are like strangers. We don't talk about one another's problems anymore. We go our separate ways and meet at the dinner table occasionally. Is this why we came to Dominica, Bruce?'

Bruce could not ignore the look of supplication on the faces of those dearest to him. He felt enraged by the thought of anyone attempting to molest or otherwise harass his wife or daughter. 'Has anyone been harassing you, San?'

'No, dad,' Sandra assured him, 'but I don't like people calling you a racist.' She emphasised her last word to indicate the contempt with which she viewed racism.

'I am not a racist, San, but I am not fond of black people,' Bruce confided.

'Why?' Sandra felt hurt. 'What's wrong with black people, dad? I find them very nice.'

'Take my advice,' Bruce warned, 'they are not to be trusted. Sure, you can talk with them, but watch how friendly you become with them.'

'Don't you trust Mabes, dad?' Sandra pursued. 'I've made some very close friendships with black girls and boys.'

'What!' Bruce raised his voice. 'Are there boys attending the convent?'

'No, dad,' Sandra laughed, 'the boys I know are friends of Mark.'

Bruce sighed in relief. 'Anyway, you ought to be very careful how you treat them. Don't be too trusting of them,' he said finally.

Betty leaned back against the headboard keenly observing the exchange between her husband and daughter. She knew the truth was only half told and could not resist the urge to set the record straight. She felt the time was right to reveal the truth to Sandra. To keep her in the dark, any longer, was to create more confusion later. 'Sandra wanted to know why you trust Mable,' Betty reintroduced the topic.

'Yes, dad,' Sandra confirmed, 'she is black. So?'

'Mable's different.' Bruce paused to think of an appropriate response. 'I grew up with Mabes. She was like a big sister to me. Colour didn't make a difference to me in those days.' He paused once more to consider his next thought.

Sandra took the opportunity to ask, 'Does colour make a difference now?'

'I am afraid it does, San,' Bruce acknowledged. 'As you grow up and gain experience about them, you realise black people don't like us. We have dominated them for so long that they will stop at nothing to take revenge for all those years of slavery we put them through. So we must be on our guard at all times. That's why they can't be trusted.'

'I read about the Black Power movement in America,' Sandra shared. 'They are fighting for equal treatment and opportunity, not for revenge. And so they should,' she added. 'Why should the colour of someone's skin be used to deny them equal rights in their country?'

'I have not seen a thread of revenge in Mable's treatment of us,' Betty commented. 'All her actions are protective of us. She loves us, Bruce, as if we were her family.'

'As I said, Mable is different,' Bruce repeated.

'What about Eugene, dad?'

'He is a perfect example of a traitor,' Bruce replied instantly. 'He is at the root of all the problems we are having at Riversdale right now. My father and uncle trusted him, now he is taking his revenge. He made the workers join the union, and led the strike.' Bruce spoke angrily, returning to his theme of trust as the root cause of the problem at Riversdale.

'Do you hate black people, dad?' Sandra was reacting to her father's anger at Eugene.

[120]

Bruce looked at his daughter. He realised the tone in which he spoke could indicate hatred. But he stopped long enough to consider Sandra's question. 'Not all, only those who have betrayed my trust. Eugene is one of them.'

'I think we had better start making plans to return to England, Bruce,' Betty suggested. She eased up to a more comfortable position, grimacing in pain.

'Why, mom?' Sandra asked anxiously.

'Shall I tell her, Bruce, or will you?' Betty looked him in the eye. 'I think it's time she knew, don't you?'

'What are you talking about?' Bruce was at a loss.

'I have sat here, in pain, listening to you tell San about trust as the cause of the troubles at Riversdale. You and I know that is not where the real problem lies. Sandra is eighteen, and mature enough to understand the basis of your true feelings about black people. Time we shared this with our daughter. If you won't, I will.'

Bruce darted bitter eyes at Betty as the painful memory of his father's sexual encounter with Margaret flashed before him. 'What good will it serve?'

'She needs to understand, like I do,' Betty held her ground. 'I have promised to tell her the truth if you won't.'

'So what is so terrible that I can't know?' Sandra felt separated from the discussion about her right to know. She looked at her father, then her mother.

Bruce moved to the window and gazed at the settling dusk. The sky was red with speeding clouds coloured by the rays of the setting sun.

'When your father was twelve years old...' Betty began to reveal the long promised secret.

Bruce froze, wheeled about and left the room, banging the door furiously behind him. He opened the door to the courtyard, breathed deeply, then stepped out into the cool evening air.

CHAPTER THIRTEEN

BETTY KNOWLES was relaxing on the sofa in the living room when Sandra returned from school. 'Good afternoon, mom,' Sandra greeted. 'How is your back?'

'Fine. How was school?'

'Okay,' Sandra replied.

Betty observed the worried frowns on her daughter's brow. 'So why the long face? Are the students still bothering you about dad?'

'Not today.' Sandra sat heavily on the easy chair opposite the sofa, dropping her school bag at her feet. She gazed down at the floor, not concealing her sullen face.

'Well, are you going to share your problem with your mother?' Betty encouraged.

'Mom,' Sandra began, 'I don't think you will understand.' She avoided the issue.

'All right,' Betty accepted, 'you can talk it over with your father. You always preferred to discuss things with him, anyway.'

'That's not true,' Sandra objected. 'I always discuss personal things with you.' Sandra felt uncomfortable, and grabbed her bag to leave the room.

'Do you really think I would not understand, San?' Betty asked gently. Somehow, she felt her daughter needed to talk.

'No, mom,' Sandra admitted. 'What I meant was that it is a delicate matter which you and dad would object to. So, it seemed pointless discussing it.'

'Are you falling in love, San?' Betty was direct. From experience, she recognised the signs of young love.

[123]

Sandra's sudden change of expression betrayed her secret. She smiled, yet there was a sadness in her eyes which reflected the concern in her heart. Then, her smile gave way to laughter in an attempt to cover the pink blush beneath her tanned face.

'Is it Mark?' Betty asked smiling.

'Mark!' Sandra exclaimed with more laughter, which slowly subsided as the full significance of her mother's assumption became clear. Of course, her parents would expect her to relate amorously only with a young man of her colour, in view of her father's attitude toward black people.

'Well?' Betty was anxious. 'Is it?'

'No, mom.' Sandra shook her head slowly. 'It's ... he's black.'

Betty sat up instantly from her reclining position. 'Black?' she repeated, whispering deliberately to avoid being overheard by Mable in the kitchen.

Sandra nodded. She sensed the fear in her mother's voice. Fear that her father would be outraged by the thought of his daughter falling in love with the very object of his hatred. Fear that his deep-seated wounds would be wrenched asunder once more to bring added pain and torment. She was his only child, the object of all his love and caring. This would be the ultimate betrayal, far more destructive than the seeming rejection he suffered by his father's intimacy with Margaret.

'Well!' Betty breathed a heavy sigh. 'I don't know what to say. This is the last thing I expected to hear. Well!' She shrugged her shoulders. 'Who is he? Do we know his parents? Is he very dark, or light-skinned? Have you been seeing him for some time? Oh dear,' Betty said anxiously, 'what will your father say?'

'Don't worry, mom,' Sandra sat by her mother's side. 'We only just met. He is the kind of person daddy would like, if he were white. He is very intelligent, ambitious, very handsome, well-mannered, and wants to become a doctor.'

'If he were white!' Betty repeated. 'Did you hear what you just said? If he were white!'

'Yes, mom,' Sandra said calmly, 'that's the only problem, and it is dad's problem.' Sandra took her mother's hand. 'I like John

[124]

very much. We have been seeing each other for several weeks now. He is Mark's friend, and comes from a well-respected family, the Deshauts.'

'So, how serious are you two?' Betty asked.

'How do you mean?' Sandra did not understand.

'I mean how deeply involved are you? Do you hold hands? Do you kiss him? And, what else?' Betty was visibly embarrassed by her own interrogation. She was new at this, but realised her daughter was no longer the innocent child under her maternal protection. She knew what it was like growing up without a mother. There were times when she wanted to talk with someone she could confide in, and share the teething problems that all young lovers encounter.

Sandra was still holding her mother's hand when Mable walked in. 'Afternoon, Miss Sandra,' she greeted. 'Didn' know you come back awready. All you want tea now? It ready.'

'Sure, Mable,' Betty said, but she was more interested in her daughter's answers to her probing questions. She turned to Sandra when Mable left. 'Well? How serious are you two?'

'Mom,' Sandra addressed her mother squarely, 'I am a full-grown woman at eighteen. You have brought me up to be responsible, decent and moral. I will not let you down, okay?' She squeezed her mother's hand. 'Yes, we have kissed, but that's as far as we will let it go. John is very responsible, too. He respects me, and will do nothing to embarrass me. As I said we've only just met a few weeks ago.'

Betty looked at her daughter with pride in her teary eyes. How she wished, as a young girl, she could have shared such thoughts with her mother. 'I believe you, dear,' she said. 'I will trust you to behave like the lady I know you are, and I believe John will love you the more for it.' They hugged each other just when Mable brought in the afternoon tea.

'Hm, hm,' Mable smiled, 'it so nice to see daughter an' modder huggin'.'

'We should do it more often,' Betty replied, and was about to fill their teacups when Bruce's car pulled into the driveway. 'You'd better get another cup, Mabes.'

[125]

Mable wobbled her way to the kitchen while Betty and Sandra looked at each other. Their thoughts were, undoubtedly, on the kind of reaction to be expected from Bruce when he learnt of his daughter's involvement with a black man.

'Let's not tell your father about this, unless it becomes serious,' Betty suggested.

'All right, mom,' Sandra agreed.

'Hi folks,' Bruce greeted cheerfully, then asked Sandra, 'How was school?'

'Fine, dad, fine.' Sandra was smiling to what seemed her usual warm and understanding father. But would he understand when he heard that she was in love with a black man?

Sandra sat with Debra at the rear of the school listening eagerly to her friend relate how she spent the weekend with her boyfriend, Daniel. 'When are we going to the beach again, Debie?' Sandra asked suddenly.

'Any Sunday that we are free. Next Sunday, if you like,' Debra suggested, 'but it is revision time. We need all the weekends before exams to catch up.'

'You are right,' Sandra agreed. 'But it's such a long time since we went out as a group,' she lamented, 'I think it's time we did it again.'

'August Monday is only two weeks off,' Debra reminded. 'Don't forget the school dance.'

'Oh, that's right!' Sandra shouted ecstatically. 'I almost forgot. In fact, I have not even asked my father for permission yet.' Sandra smiled as she imagined herself in John's arms on the dance floor. 'I hope John likes the way I dance,' she said softly.

'We don't really dance, you know, Sandra,' Debra laughed. 'How can you dance when he holds you so close? You know, it's more like making love,' she whispered. 'We hardly move. We just stand there squeezing and rubbing against each other, swaying to the music. Some of us even kiss while dancing.'

'What!' Sandra exclaimed, so loudly, that several pairs of eyes turned in their direction. She blushed, and both started laughing at the embarrassing moment which followed. Then, Sandra continued softly, 'You mean some of them kiss right there in the presence of everybody?'

'Sure! I did it once, but it was a bit dark. The lights were turned low and the music was so romantic that for a moment I forgot where I was. I only knew I was in Danny's arms and his lips were on mine.' Debie's voice mellowed as she recalled the experience.

Sandra smiled pleasantly. 'It must have been lovely. I wonder if I would have the courage to do that?'

'You don't need courage, because it just happens. Your eyes are closed. You feel secure in his arms and you think of nothing else but being in love with the most wonderful man in the world.'

'I see what you mean,' Sandra mused. 'I see what you mean.'

'So, how is it going with you and John?' Debra changed the subject.

'Would you believe I told my mother about him?' Sandra opened her eyes excitedly.

'Really? And what did she say?' Debra asked curiously.

'It is strange, but, she knew I was in love before I told her,' Sandra observed, 'but I couldn't help laughing when she thought it was Mark.'

'Mark?' Debra repeated, and laughed. But her laughter was brief as she quickly realised it was natural for Sandra's mother to think that. 'Well, I guess it would be expected, because he is white.'

'That is exactly what I thought.' Sandra said, 'And was she shocked when she learned that he was black! She was more concerned about what my father would think, because he is not very fond of black people, as he put it.'

'Really?' Debra said softly, examining her own chocolate skin. 'So, it's true he is racist?'

Sandra's face flushed immediately. 'He is not racist,' she said harshly. 'How can you, of all people, suggest that?'

'Sorry, Sandra,' Debra apologised immediately. 'I was only asking because of what you said about he not being fond of black people.'

'Well, that's what it is.' Sandra felt embarrassed by her tone,

[127]

and smiled to her friend. 'It's a long story, Debie, which started when my father was just a boy. I'll tell you about it one day.'

'Are you going to tell him about John?'

'Mom and I decided not to at this time. But if we should get serious later on, then we will tell him.'

'I think that's wise, Sandra,' Debra observed. 'I, too, have a problem with my people, not just my family. I cannot bring Danny home as my boyfriend. The Carib culture is very traditional about mixing the races. If I were to marry Danny, I would lose my inheritance and my entire connection with the Carib race.'

'Well, that's silly! That's worse than being racist. Your people would be disowning you,' Sandra was appalled.

'However, if it were the other way around, and Danny was Carib and I black, it would be okay,' Debra laughed.

'So what's the difference?' Sandra asked. 'Wouldn't the races be mixed then?'

'It's a male-dominated culture, San. Women are pushed into the background,' Debra lamented.

'When you think about it, we have the same problem,' Sandra observed. 'The white race tends to reject those of its members who marry blacks as well, both male and female. Isn't that stupid?'

'That means you can expect your father to reject John if you get serious.'

'Yes, I expect so,' Sandra agreed. 'But one thing is certain. No matter how much I love my father, he will not decide for me who I fall in love with.'

'That's good,' Debra supported. After all, it's your life, not his.' They were both nodding their heads in agreement when the bell rang to conclude the recess. As they rose to return to classes, Debie said, 'I hope you both fall in love, San.'

'I hope so, too,' Sandra smiled happily.

CHAPTER FOURTEEN

FOR SEVERAL weeks, working conditions at Riversdale Plantations were pleasant and peaceful. Bruce remained aloof in his managerial tasks, leaving all else to the three field supervisors. He spent more time at home, too, and tended to be more relaxed. He even found time to sit and share tea with his family.

This Saturday evening, he was preparing to take Betty to the Red Rose Club dance. His happy frame of mind was evidenced by his outrageous singing in the shower which provoked fits of laughter from Mable.

'Lord, have mercy!' Mable exclaimed, turning to Sandra who was helping her in the kitchen. 'Your fadder singin' or he quarrelin' wif a zombie?' she asked jokingly.

'I guess it must be with Beelzebub himself!' Sandra laughed.

'Well, den, B'elzebub in plenty trouble wif Brucie tonight!' Mable folded in still more laughter.

Meanwhile, Betty was sitting before the mirror in her bedroom applying the finishing touches to her make-up. She smiled when she remembered how long it was since Bruce had taken her dancing. Then, her countenance turned to sadness as she let her thoughts dwell on her drinking problem. 'That's not the way,' she muttered. 'Surely, you can use your time more usefully in helping others,' she said to her image in the mirror.

Just then, Bruce walked in with a towel wrapped around his waist. 'Love,' he said, 'are you serious about doing volunteer work?'

Betty turned abruptly and looked at her husband strangely. 'Now, that must be telepathy,' she remarked, 'because I was just now thinking about that. Do you remember how frequently this used to happen in England?' She stood up and approached him. 'It's like the old days again, love.'

Bruce looked at his wife and smiled provocatively. 'Bet you can't tell what I am thinking right now.'

Betty laughed, then backed away. 'Oh no, you don't,' she said, 'I spent too much time on my make-up. You aren't going to ruin it, at least, not yet.'

In the kitchen Sandra was watching how Mable plaited the dough which she laid on banana leaf, ready to be placed in the oven. 'Let me try the next one, Mabes.'

Mable watched proudly as Sandra demonstrated her ability to learn. 'Yes, mam,' Mable congratulated, 'you goin' to make a good wife, Miss Sandra.'

'I hope so,' Sandra smiled as she thought of John Deshaut. 'I want to learn how to prepare all Caribbean dishes. Will you teach me?'

'Yes, Miss Sandra,' Mable promised without hesitation. 'I teach Miss Maria an' Miss Bella, but dey never have time for cookin',' Mable regretted.

'I will,' Sandra said, 'because my husband will be black.'

Mable turned sharply to face a smiling Sandra, but Sandra saw a furious Mable, causing her own face to transform slowly from one of happiness through seriousness, confusion and apprehension. 'What you say, chil'?' Mable punctuated.

Sandra hesitated and wondered to herself, 'Did I offend Mable? What did I say to offend her?' Her mind raced to try to make sense from a confused situation.

'What's the matter, Mabes? Did I say something to offend you?' She raised her hands enquiringly.

'Yes, you did!' Mable rebuked, 'But, I don' fink dis is what you want to say.'

Sandra nodded. 'Yes, Mabes, this is what I meant to say. I am going to marry a black man.'

Mable stiffened, thrust her chest forward as she inhaled deeply,

[130]

then turned away from Sandra and walked to the window. She was at a loss for words.

Sandra did not understand Mable's behaviour. Why should she be upset at such news? 'Mabes,' Sandra called out pleadingly, 'I am sorry if I upset you. I thought you would be pleased to hear that I am in love with a black man.'

'You what?' Mable reacted suddenly, shocked by the revelation. 'You don' know what you sayin', chil'! You don' know! You still in school, an' you talkin' about sinful fings. No! No! You don' know!'

'Mabes, I am not a child,' Sandra protested. 'Of course I know about these things. I'm eighteen years old, you know.'

'A black man?' Mable asked indignantly.

'What's wrong with a black man?' Sandra was curious.

'What wrong wif a black man?' Mable repeated the question. 'What you know about dem? On'y one fing dey after,' she said flatly.

'Mable, I am surprised at you,' Sandra chastised. 'You are a black woman, a very beautiful and gentle black woman. I have never met a nicer and more caring person than you. I am sure your father was a black man, wasn't the?'

'Yes, he is,' Mable replied quickly, 'but, he is a good man,' she added, placing her hands on her hips.

'The man I love is a good man, too,' Sandra said, also placing her hands on her hips, imitating Mable.

Mable smiled and shook her head hopelessly. 'Before, is Mr Charles, now, is you,' she muttered. 'Why you not lovin' a white man instead?' Mable asked bluntly.

Sandra was shocked at this unexpected question. This is the question her father would ask. From him one would understand the racial preference, but, coming from Mable, Sandra was confused. 'Mabes,' Sandra spoke softly and deliberately, choosing her words carefully. 'Is it wrong for me to fall in love with a black man?'

'It not wrong, but it not good for you,' Mable replied immediately.

'Why is it bad?' Sandra pursued.

[131]

'Because dey no good. If you lovin' a black man, black people fink you no good, too. Dey callin' you white trash. Dat's what dey call Miss Emily. And you is no white trash, Miss Sandra,' Mable was emphatic.

Sandra smiled at the manner in which Mable expressed herself. She knew Mable was stereotyping.

'You laughin'?' Mable asked when she observed the smiling response from Sandra. 'You fink is joke? You know what happen to Miss Emily? She get pregnant an' dey sen' her to Barbados. Dat's what you want dem to do wif you?' Mable was clearly concerned for Sandra.

'Oh, no, Mabes,' Sandra explained, 'I don't think it is a joke. But I think you are looking at all black men alike. Of course, some will be bad, but not all. Just like some white men are bad, but not all. You understand?' Sandra tried to bring some perspective to Mable's sweeping condemnation of black men. 'You said your father was a good man, so all black men cannot be bad.' She paused to see if Mable agreed.

'Well,' Mable said finally, 'some black men awright, but I still say dey after one fing.'

'What thing?' Sandra probed.

Mable returned quickly to her dough and continued to knead, obviously embarrassed by Sandra's question. 'You don' know?' She asked shyly.

'No, I don't.' Sandra pretended ignorance, because she had heard the comments from white schoolmates in London concerning the sexual obsession of blacks. But she had never heard a black person admit to it.

'Den, why you fink Miss Emily get pregnant?' Mable hinted.

Sandra laughed and Mable smiled. After this exchange, without words, Sandra decided not to pursue the subject any further. But, she remained convinced that Mable was closed-minded on the question of inter-racial love and marriage. However, Sandra became curious about Emily. 'Tell me about Emily,' she started, just when her mother walked into the kitchen to show her dress and make-up.

'Oh, Lord! You so pretty!' Mable screamed, raised her floured hands in the air and clapped in admiration. A cloud of flour dust filled the air before her face and they all laughed at the spectacle.

Betty spun around to display her beautifully flowered, knee-length, flared skirt which bounced from side to side with her thick, colourful petticoat. Her red-dotted, white blouse tapered precisely to her small waist and was held on her bare bosom, precariously, by two red strings tied at her shoulders. Her outfit matched her lipstick which left no doubt about its sensuous intent.

'Yes, mom, you look beautiful,' Sandra approved. 'And where is Prince Charming?'

'Here I am,' Bruce announced, entering to show off his bright red shirt, lined with white lace at the front, and resting gently on cream, flannel trousers.

'You look dashing, dad,' Sandra praised. 'You and mom are going to be the centre of attraction at the ball.'

'Thank you, darlings,' Bruce courtesied. 'Now, my princess, shall we depart before the clock strikes twelve?' He adapted from *Cinderella*.

Mable and Sandra watched Bruce and Betty leave. When the jeep's rear lights disappeared from view, Mable remarked, 'He jus' like his fadder.'

The notes from the steel band rang louder and clearer as the jeep approached Red Rose Club. Betty began bobbing her head and tapping her shoes to the beat of the well-known song, '*Matilda*'. She joined in the refrain.

'You really like this kind of music, don't you?' Bruce observed.

'Yes. It's alive, stimulating, and makes you want to dance,' Betty explained while she continued her movement.

'Whenever I hear it, I think of our farewell party in London,' Bruce recalled. 'I remember Simone, in particular, and what she said to me.'

'What *did* she say, Bruce?' Betty asked. 'You never did tell me.'

'Now that I think of it, I realise that I overreacted to a perfectly innocent and funny remark.' Bruce shook his head. 'All she said was that I would be so captivated by the sexy, black beauties on the island that I would forget my friends in London.'

Betty laughed heartily at that remark. 'She was obviously drunk and didn't mean it literally.'

'I know now. But at the time I felt repulsed by the suggestion.' Bruce sounded apologetic.

'So now that you are here, are you captivated?' Betty teased.

'Betty, please,' Bruce implored.

'I find nothing repulsive about the people of the island.' Betty became thoughtful. 'On the contrary, they are very friendly, polite, helpful and full of joy.'

Bruce did not comment on his wife's opinion. He respected her liberal views, but felt that without personal experience, as he had, it was easy to give them the benefit of the doubt.

'Sandra mixes with them every day,' Betty continued, 'and she finds them just as normal as the white children at her school in London. She has quite a few friends already.' Betty looked at her husband before she said, 'We should not be surprised if she falls in love with one of them.'

Bruce stiffened at this remark causing the jeep to jump forward as his foot jerked the accelerator involuntarily. 'Don't be absurd, Betty!' He admonished. 'Sandra knows how I feel about black people. You made sure of that. So she wouldn't dare fall in love with one of them!' Bruce's face turned sour at the suggestion. 'How could you even think such a thing?' He felt hurt.

'I am only being realistic, love,' Betty spoke softly. 'She's eighteen, you know. We can't very well tell her not to associate with black male friends, nor with whom she should fall in love.' Betty realised that Bruce would find out about John Deshaut, sooner or later. It was wise, therefore, to prepare him for the inevitable.

'Betty,' Bruce raised his right hand, 'let's drop the subject. We will deal with it if, and when, it happens, which I know will be never.'

'Fine with me, love,' Betty shrugged her shoulders, 'but it seems to me you do not know your daughter very well.' She sighed. 'As a matter of fact, you both are much alike in many ways, particularly in having your own way.'

Bruce smiled at Betty's comparison, signifying his approval, and held his smile right up to the parking lot of the Red Rose Club. The music ended just when he helped Betty to the ground.

'Good Lord!' Betty cried. 'The place is crowded! Listen to the noise!'

'Yes, sir, it is loud,' Bruce agreed. 'I think it is the music, though. The sound of the steel drums may still be vibrating in their ears so they become hard of hearing for a while, and tend to speak louder.'

'That probably explains it,' Betty said, 'or else, they are emptying the bar very quickly.'

Bruce laughed at Betty's light-heartedness, then caressed her shoulders warmly. 'You are really very beautiful tonight, love,' he complimented. 'I hope these lecherers keep their paws off you.'

Betty laughed, slipped her hand around his waist and said, 'With you to protect me, love, who would dare?' They laughed and turned toward the entrance.

Sandra lay on the sofa with her feet on the headrest. In the subdued light of the living room her smile was seductive and her voice mellow. She clutched the telephone receiver close to her breast as if it were John himself who lay in her arms. 'I do love you, John,' she said, 'but do you really love me?'

'How can you doubt that?' John's voice broke on the telephone.

'Because you don't want to come over,' Sandra was unforgiving. 'If you loved me, you would want to be with me at every opportunity we get.'

'Sandra,' John pleaded, 'I am dying to come, but not so secretly. Suppose your parents return and find me with you, I couldn't forgive myself.'

'My mother knows all about you,' Sandra revealed. 'Very soon, my father will know about you too. So why should you be afraid if they find you here?' Sandra paused for his answer, but John was silent. A few moments passed by before Sandra called, 'John! Are you there, John?'

'Yes, Sandra,' John answered, 'I'll come, against my better judgement.'

'I'll look out for you.' She swung her legs down to the floor, sitting up at the same time. She smiled happily, stood, then replaced the receiver on its cradle at the bar. She looked at the clock on the wall which showed ten after nine. She was aware that students at John's school were not allowed out at night without parental escort. 'Only one hour left to curfew,' she whispered, and hurried to the kitchen window. Mable had retired early.

The night air in the valley was fresh, cooled by the descending mountain breezes and the rushing Woodbridge river. In the distance, the light from a bicycle moved from side to side as the rider avoided the potholes in the dirt road. Then, the light turned into the access road to Knowles Gardens. Sandra's heart skipped a beat. 'This must be John,' she whispered to herself. The rider dismounted. As he got nearer, Sandra recognised him. Quietly, she ran out of the kitchen entrance and down the steps to greet him.

'Where can I hide my bicycle?' John whispered.

'At the back, here,' Sandra pointed, leading him by the hand. 'Let's sit out by the pool. We can't be seen from the road, and, if my parents should return unexpectedly, you can leave without being seen and I can enter quite innocently.'

'I think you are crazy, Sandra, but, I love you.' John pulled her into his arms and kissed her tenderly. Sandra was quickly aroused by his close embrace, moaning passionately as she kissed him back. Then, they both eased down gently onto the foam mat by the poolside, locked in each other's arms.

It seemed like eternity before Sandra and John finally relaxed their embrace. They rolled on their backs to gaze at the star-lit sky, still holding hands. 'Isn't it wonderful to be in love?' Sandra whispered.

'Marvellous!' John replied. 'They say love makes the world go round, and I believe that.'

'I'm glad love brought us together, John,' Sandra turned to embrace him once more. 'Please don't ever leave me, no matter what obstacles come our way.'

'That goes for me, too,' John replied as he looked into her pleading and worried eyes. He kissed them, drawing her closer. 'You are the most wonderful thing that has ever happened to me, Sandra, and I am not about to let you go.'

'You are my first love, John,' Sandra revealed, 'and I don't want any other.' She kissed him hungrily as he drew his body against hers. They breathed heavily from their anxiety to express their love for each other. Their lips separated, and John rested his face on Sandra's bosom. She shivered slightly, surrendering her breasts to his soft moist lips. 'I love you, John,' she cried breathlessly.

'You have no idea how much I want you right now, San,' John lifted his head to see teary eyes and smiling lips. He kissed her tears and then her lips. 'You will never know how much I love you.' John shook his head and smiled.

'I know,' Sandra said calmly, 'you love me enough not to take advantage of my weakness.'

John looked into her eyes, smiled, then asked, 'How did you know that is what I was thinking?'

'Because I, too, was hungry for you,' Sandra confessed. 'This is the first time I felt this way, love. I was just aching inside, not knowing what was happening to me. I was feeling wonderful when you kissed my breast and didn't want you to stop. I was helpless, then, and you didn't take advantage of me. My tears were tears of joy, from knowing just how much you love me.'

He drew her closer to him. 'I believe we were destined for each other, San,' John said. 'Let us keep our love pure till the day we become one. Would you like that?'

'Oh, I would like that very much, John, if you want it,' Sandra agreed.

'I do, San,' John promised, 'and, believe me, you are my only love. I will seek no other till the day you want me no more.'

'That day will never come, John,' Sandra held him close, 'not even if my father tries to break us apart.'

[137]

'I'm glad you feel this way,' John said. 'I would not want to be responsible for destroying your relationship with your father.' He glanced at his watch. 'Oh-oh, it's past curfew! I better be going.'

They stood up hurriedly, embraced and kissed goodbye. But when Sandra opened her eyes, her body froze. Mable was standing at her bedroom window, looking down upon the love scene below. Without a word to John, Sandra escorted him to his bicycle and waved as he sped on his way.

When Sandra returned, Mable was standing at the bottom of the stairs. Sandra approached her with a smile, but she met an angry, twisted, hostile face, with piercing eyes and flaring nostrils. As Sandra looked upon this show of utter disapproval from this affable and warm person she had grown to love she began to cry suddenly, then ran to her room. For a moment, Mable stood, perplexed by Sandra's unusual behaviour, then turned and followed her.

Sandra lay across her bed sobbing, and clinging on to her pillow. Mable was no longer angry, but concerned. She stood by the bed looking at the pitiful sight of a young woman in love. Then she sat on the bed beside Sandra who immediately threw herself into Mable's arms. 'I love him, Mabes, I love him,' she cried out between sobs.

Mable became even more confused. Her instincts dictated that she should on the one hand console Sandra, and on the other admonish her. Seized by these conflicting demands, Mable's arms remained suspended in mid-air, trembling from her struggle within. Slowly, she succumbed to the power of love, and embraced Sandra, gently. 'Is awright, Miss Sandra, is awright.' She rocked her, back and forth, like a baby, repeating, 'Is awright, don' cry, Miss Sandra, is awright.' Mable's eyes filled with tears, but her smile was a joyous one.

The dancing area was packed with revellers. It was hot and smoky. Sweat glistened from their faces, dripping down their necks and turning their well-groomed shirts into wet rags, clinging to their bodies and twisting in whichever way their torsos went in response to the calypso beat. Bruce and Betty threw their arms in the air, rocking their bodies in gay abandon. Then, they hugged to continue their rocking in tight embrace. Finally, like everyone else, they raised their hands and voices in applause when the music ended.

The laughter was resounding as the revellers were returning to their seats. Bruce and Betty were sharing a table with new-found friends who had ordered drinks for the group. The black waiter was placing the drinks on the table when James Compton approached him and said, 'Hey, boy, you serving dis man?' He pointed at Bruce. 'Don' do dat,' he imitated the creole vernacular. 'He's de boy, now, at Riversdale. You didn' hear dat?'

'No sir,' the black waiter answered out of respect, but visibly embarrassed by the insinuation.

There was instant silence in the area surrounding the table, causing the noise to shift to one side of the lounge. But, like a wave, the silence swept its way across the room leaving in its wake a whisper here and a rustle there.

All eyes were now upon James Compton who was jeering at Bruce, drunkenly. 'Is it true, my white friend, that you gave in to those black bastards on your estate, eh? Is it true?' James leaned forward, placing his hands on the table to steady himself.

'You are drunk, you fool,' Bruce retorted. 'Go on home before you make an ass of yourself.'

'It's you who have made bloody asses of all of us,' James pointed a shaking finger at Bruce. 'What else are you going to give them, eh? Your wife and daughter?'

With the swiftness of a mountain cat pouncing on its prey, Bruce lunged forward across the table to register a solid right fist upon the open jaws of James Compton. The impact sounded like a cracking cricket bat, dry from lack of oiling. The table shifted, and so did the crowd. James sprawled across the adjacent table, spilling drinks, and sending glasses crashing to the floor. When he staggered up, Bruce was standing right before him ready to repeat the dosage. But he was restrained by strong hands. And so was James, who was escorted out of the club.

Betty rushed to her husband's side and embraced him warmly.

'You should have given him another one for Sandra, too,' she spewed. 'Who the dickens does he think he is?!'

'He had it coming to him for a long time, Bruce,' his table companion said when they resumed their seats. 'Ever since that black fellow refused to marry his pregnant sister, he has hated them with a passion. Personally, I can't say I have much use for him. He embarrasses the white community all the time. He is tolerated here only because he is white.'

'He is like the *black sheep* of the white community, so to speak,' another companion remarked. 'He has been in court several times for offences against blacks – assaults, harassment, provocation, trespass, you name it, he's done it.'

'It baffles me that the blacks have not retaliated in same measure,' the first companion observed. 'They are certainly very tolerant and forgiving.'

'It's their Christian upbringing, I say,' the other added.

Just then, the steel band began to play, harmonising a love song which aroused tender feelings in Betty. 'Let's dance, love,' she took Bruce's hand and led him to the centre of the dance floor. She embraced him fully with both arms, looked up into his eyes and said, 'I love you, Bruce Knowles, and I'm proud of you.'

Bruce embraced her warmly and kissed her auburn hair. His thoughts briefly returned to their courting days. He smiled, then kissed her cheek. He sighed heavily as several thoughts crowded his mind all at once. But one seemed to be nagging him more than the rest – James Compton's attitude. 'But for the grace of God, there goes Bruce Knowles,' he thought. He was seeing for the first time what destructive effect racial hatred can have on the individual. James Compton seemed to have suffered the same kind of humiliation that he had suffered, involving a loved member of his family and a black person. For James it was his sister, for him, his mother.

Betty squeezed her husband with emotion, responding to the sweet melody of the steel band. She looked into his eyes and smiled, and again, he kissed her cheek. 'Are you getting tired, love?' She asked.

'No, why?'

'You seemed so distant a while ago,' she replied, 'I thought maybe the music was boring you.'

'No,' Bruce assured her, 'the music is romantic, it brought me back to our early days. We were so happy then, remember?'

'I do, and I'm still very happy,' she added. 'Aren't you?' Betty looked up into his eyes once more.

'Of course, I am,' Bruce replied. 'In fact, I am being reminded how fortunate I am in having you and San. And I am beginning to realise something else which I must be careful about.'

'What's that, love?'

'It has to do with me,' Bruce was evasive. 'It is something better discussed at home. But let's just say that tonight's incident with James has opened my eyes.'

The music continued and they danced to their heart's content. As the night progressed, Betty felt the warmth of her husband's embraces infuse her being just like the old days. Could he be changing? Betty smiled pleasantly.

CHAPTER FIFTEEN

I T WAS August Monday. The hurricane season was in full
swing. Heavy rains, high winds and frightening thunder-
storms were the order of the day. Sandra was at the Grammar
School dance with her friends, while Bruce and Betty sat in
their living room, with Mable, planning a party for their friends.
Mable was very excited at the idea, for it was a long time indeed
since Knowles Gardens hosted their last memorable social
gatherings.

'For de las' party, Mr Henry get a "jing-ping" ban' from
Giraudel.' Mable's eyes widened with excitement and she laughed
happily. 'An', everybody dancin', Miss Betty!'

'What kind of music do they play?' Betty asked with unbridled
curiosity.

'All kin' of music, mam,' Mable assured her. 'Dey playin'
calypso, dey playin' mazook, dey playin' belaire, an' quadril. Any
kin' of music you want, dey playin'.'

Betty smiled to her husband with eyes begging for clarification.
'I know about calypso, but, mazook and belaire? Do you know
about them, love?'

'Probably the local dances,' Bruce guessed. 'When I was a boy,
I remember seeing these local dances performed in the rural
districts. Is that right, Mabes?'

'You right, Brucie,' Mable said fondly. 'I rem'ber dem, too. All
of us goin' up to de village when is festival time. Dey have plenty
food, big concert an' dancin'. An' is "jing-ping" dat playin','
Mable recalled vividly.

'Well,' Betty smiled at their enthusiasm, 'it sounds interesting and a lot of fun. Do you think you could get in touch with the band from Giraudel for us, Mable?'

'Eugie know dem,' Mable said. 'But I not seein' Eugie dese days. He not comin' here again. You have to ask him, Brucie.'

Betty detected a note of sadness in Mable's voice. 'Yes, that's very true, Bruce,' Betty agreed. 'Why does Eugene keep away these days?'

'I guess he has no business here,' Bruce suggested. 'Or, probably, he thinks he is not welcome because of his involvement in the strike.'

'*Is* he welcome, Bruce?' Betty asked bluntly.

'Of course. I have not prevented him from coming.'

'Do you think he does not want to upset you by coming?'

'As far as I am concerned, the strike is over,' Bruce declared. 'Our relationship is purely businesslike. If he wants to visit Mable he is welcome to do so.'

'Tell him, for me, I want to see him, Brucie,' Mable urged. 'He call me on de phone de odder day, an' when I a'ks him what I do dat he not comin' to see me again, he say he busy, busy, but comin' soon. But...' Mable shrugged her shoulders to show her disappointment.

'I'll tell him for you, Mabes,' Bruce smiled, touching her on the shoulder. 'I'll tell him how much you miss him, too.'

'Thank you, Brucie,' Mable beamed a broad smile.

'Well, that settles it,' Betty concluded. 'We will get the "jing-ping" band. Now, what about food, Mabes?'

The very popular Casimir Brothers band always drew large crowds of onlookers wherever they played. It was no exception, today, at the Grammar School. The band was pouring forth sweet, calypso music through the open windows on Hillsborough Street. Several in the crowd were dancing on the wet pavement and sidewalks, while others were content to watch the dancers within.

Sandra was laughing constantly as she tried, without much success, to learn the intricate steps John was teaching her. She opted, instead, for the easy two-step, and the close embrace. This was her first real dance, and at eighteen, she felt awkward. Her friend, Debie, was dancing with such rhythmical expression that Sandra remarked, 'I wish I could dance like Debie. She makes it look easy, but I know it's not.'

'It's not,' John agreed, 'but it becomes easy with practice.' He smiled at Sandra, then added, 'For your first time, you are doing very well, San. Here, we start dancing from childhood. Music is in our bones. So, don't worry. I intend taking you to all the dances possible, and very soon, you will be dancing like Debie.'

Sandra laughed. 'I doubt it,' she shook her head, 'but I would love to go to every dance with you.'

The music stopped, and the bandleader announced a short intermission. Sandra and Debie, with their escorts, stepped outside into the fresh air. They were soon joined by Mark who took his turn to order refreshments.

'Are you enjoying it, Sandra?' Debie asked.

'Not half as much as you,' Sandra laughed. 'You are so good on your feet, I think you should be a professional dancer.'

'Better not put any ideas in her head, Sandra,' Daniel intervened, 'she is already much too conceited!'

'Shut up, you.' Debie held Daniel by the shoulder and shook him gently. He responded by embracing her and kissing her lips.

'Isn't that sweet?' Sandra observed. 'What better way to appease an angry heart?'

Mark returned with drinks, and ice creams for the ladies. 'See you all later,' he said hastily, 'I checkin' out a situation.'

The boys laughed heartily, because they knew what Mark meant. 'Good luck,' wished John.

'Let us know what happens,' shouted Daniel.

'These guys,' Debra scoffed, 'they believe we don't know what they are talking about, San.'

'Or whom, to be more exact,' Sandra added, laughing.

John and Daniel looked at each other innocently, shrugged their shoulders pretending ignorance. Debra and Sandra smiled, then burst into laughter, while John and Daniel looked on with blank faces.

'You pretenders,' Debra teased, 'Eve told us all about it, the other day. So, you see, she was checking him out as well.'

'Is Eve interested?' Daniel asked.

'I doubt it,' John interjected, 'She is too hot for Mark. She would burn him.'

'Not unlike someone I know,' Sandra added looking at her friend Debra, and holding on to John in anticipation of Debra's retaliation.

'Are you referring to me, San?' It was Debra's turn to be embarrassed.

'Well, she hasn't burnt me yet,' Daniel came to her defence. 'But what do they say about still waters?'

'They run deep,' Debra completed, 'so mind you don't get drowned, Johnny boy.'

The laughter and joking stopped when the music resumed with a tantalising and romantic melody. The captivating sound of the saxophone hypnotised their hearts and, like robots, couples filled the dance floor in close embracing.

Sandra felt wonderful as she lay her head on John's chest, then smiled when she saw Eve in Mark's arms. 'Look, John, Mark and Eve,' she looked in their direction. 'I hope they fall in love.'

'Me, too,' John agreed. 'I hope he takes her seriously. He's been too much of a playboy.'

'I think he will, because Eve told us he said he wants to go steady,' Sandra divulged, then added, 'I hope his father is not like mine.'

'What do you mean?'

'That he is more open-minded and tolerant by accepting it if Mark chooses to fall in love with a black girl,' she said bluntly.

John felt Sandra tighten her embrace, probably to reassure him that all is well with her father and their love relationship. But he knew better. He knew he had to prove to her father that he was as worthy of his daughter as any white man, if not more so. He would not want to destroy the relationship between Sandra and her father. She was young and still under parental authority, as he was. He was prepared to wait till the day Sandra became independent, and was able to make her own decisions. However,

[146]

he would continue loving her no matter what. He kissed her hair and sighed away his troubled thoughts.

Sandra looked up and smiled when his lips touched her brow. 'The music is so romantic, I feel like dancing all night,' Sandra said.

'I love you, San,' John whispered. But the tone of his voice said much more. He wanted to say he would never desert her under any circumstances. That he would always be there to comfort and protect her in time of adversity. That one day he would be hers forever.

It was already eight in the evening. Betty, Bruce and Mable were concluding their party plans. 'The big question is whom do we invite apart from our close friends?' Betty looked to her husband for suggestions.

'Don't look at me, love, you know as many as I know,' he shook his head. 'It would have been helpful if uncle had left an invitation list.'

'Dere have one in de kitchen, in de bottom draw,' Mable revealed. 'Is a ol' one Mr Henry give me when I phonin' for dere party. But, it still good.'

'Please get it, Mable,' Betty said excitedly. 'I would love to see the original guest list.'

Mable obliged, hurrying off to the kitchen.

A flash of lightning, followed by a peal of thunder disturbed the heavens and let fall heavy beads of tropical rain. 'Oh dear,' Betty exclaimed, 'I hope Sandra has no difficulty getting back home.'

'Mark did say he would be accompanying her back, did he not?' Bruce asked.

'I believe so,' Betty replied, 'but the weather is getting worse.'

Mable returned with the list which Betty took anxiously to read out the names. They were white as well as black, rich as well as poor, those in authority as well as those of common rank. As she read, she gazed occasionally at Bruce who held a frown upon his face which she did not like.

'You don't like the list Bruce,' Betty observed.

He did not answer. Instead he turned to Mable and asked, 'Have all these people been in this house at uncle's parties?'

'Yes sir, Mr Bruce,' Mable shook her head proudly, 'an' dey all welcome by Mr Henry.'

Mable was more impressed by those of importance, which she delighted in serving. But Bruce was concerned primarily with the mingling of blacks and whites. He smiled at Betty. 'I guess recognition has its price,' he nodded, 'and for my uncle it was his pride.'

Betty smiled faintly, more for respect for Mable than for approval of her husband's remarks. For she knew exactly what he meant, unlike Mable who stared at him with blind admiration and love, totally unaware of the insult he had implied about black people. Betty stopped reading the names and bowed her head shamefully, then said, 'I am tired, let's make up the list tomorrow.'

'I tired, too, mam,' Mable rose from the settee. 'I better make nightcap now. Miss Sandra comin' soon.'

When they were alone, Betty looked at her husband steadfastly. She felt a burning urge to castigate him for his unkind remark in Mable's presence.

'I know what you are thinking, love,' Bruce said, 'that I am carrying my prejudice too far. But I would have to swallow a whole lot of pride to invite these people into my home. To work with them is one thing, but to eat and be merry with them is an entirely different matter. I cannot pretend I like them by inviting them to my home.'

Just then, the mud entrance door swung open and in rushed Sandra, laughing at the condition of her umbrella, which was turned inside-out by heavy winds. 'Come in, John,' she beckoned, 'come in and meet my parents.'

Reluctantly, John stepped onto the porch, bowed shyly and muttered, 'Good evening, Mr and Mrs Knowles.'

'Mom, dad, this is a good friend of mine, John Deshaut,' Sandra introduced happily. 'He brought me home because Mark was not able to come.'

'Good evening, John,' Betty welcomed, and stretched a hand,

[148]

'I am pleased to meet you. And thank you for bringing Sandra home. Please come in.'

John was still standing on the porch, not expecting to be invited in, and remained there when he heard the stern voice of Bruce Knowles. 'Where is Mark?'

'He could not come, dad,' Sandra repeated.

'Then, why didn't you call me?' Bruce bellowed, his rage increasing by the minute. 'I would have gladly come for you instead of placing yourself in the debt of strangers.'

'It's my fault, sir,' John gallantly tried taking the blame to save Sandra any further inquisition. 'I offered to take Sandra home, since I live much closer than Mark.'

'Young man!' Bruce shouted, startling both Sandra and John. 'I did not address you. I do not know you, nor do I wish to do so. You are not welcome in my house. Please leave.'

'Dad!' Sandra protested. 'What are you saying! John is my closest friend here, and is that how you are treating him?' She turned around suddenly and ran after John who had departed with all haste.

'Sandra!' Betty called out after her daughter, running to the door. But not even the clattering thunder nor blinding lightning could stop Sandra's wounded heart from pursuing her bruised lover.

Bruce remained glued to the same position where he had uttered his damning words. His daughter's reaction was so swift and decisive that he was taken by surprise. Now, he faced the painful eyes of his wife, Betty, who began to beat wildly on her husband's chest, as she tried, unsuccessfully, to speak and cry simultaneously. Bruce tried to comfort her with an embrace, which would have been welcome under other circumstances, but, instead she pushed him aside and ran to her bedroom as her wailing erupted.

Mable appeared at the bar entrance, perplexed. She looked in the direction of the crying Betty and then at an enraged Bruce and wondered what transpired. Mable chose to attend to Betty since Bruce appeared to be the cause of her crying.

Sandra caught up with John, and embraced him in the pouring

rain, their clenched bodies silhouetted in the delayed flashes of lightning. 'I'm sorry, love, I'm sorry,' Sandra cried as she kissed him passionately.

A clap of thunder exploded overhead, causing John to embrace Sandra protectively. 'Don't cry, San,' he urged, 'please let's go back to your home. You shouldn't be out here in this weather. Your mother would be worried.'

'No, I won't,' Sandra shouted. 'I cannot forgive my father for what he did to you. He doesn't love me. He is a racist, and I hate him!'

John realised that Sandra was hurting much more than he was. They could not remain exposed to the elements. 'Come on then, let's get shelter.' He held her hand as both ran into the Botanic Gardens, across the cricket field, and into the open pavilion.

Exhausted, they let themselves fall heavily on the canvas covers for the cricket pitch. Then, Sandra rolled over towards John and said tenderly, 'I will always love you, John, no matter what. My father will not decide for me to whom I shall give my heart. I'm yours, if you still want me.' They embraced hungrily, oblivious of their drenched clothes and dripping hair. They kissed as they had never kissed before, holding each other so closely that not even the resounding thunder and fiery lightning could dislodge them.

At Knowles Gardens, Betty was asking for a drink, but Mable held her in her arms like a baby. 'Is awright, Miss Betty, Miss Sandra comin' back soon. She don' have nowhere else to go.'

'But, she is in this terrible weather with this boy, and I can't help her,' Betty cried.

'She safe wif him, mam,' Mable consoled. 'He is a good man, Miss Sandra tell me, and I believe her.'

'You think so, Mabes?' Betty was somewhat relieved.

'Yes, mam. He is a good man,' Mable repeated.

Betty stood up suddenly from her sitting position. 'I will never forgive Bruce if anything happens to Sandra,' she turned her anger upon her husband. Mable cringed at the rising wrath of Betty Knowles, and followed her out of the bedroom. Betty entered the living room where Bruce sat on the sofa, arms folded, deep in thought. 'You are a monster, an unforgiving bigot. You are so obsessed with childhood fantasies that you are blinded by the fact that your daughter is now a woman.'

Bruce raised his head slowly to look at his wife as she continued to pour venom from her tender mouth.

'Why don't you face the truth, Bruce. You are letting a twenty-five-year-old childhood jealousy poison your mind against black people. The problem is not your father or, what's her name, Margaret! *You* are the problem, Bruce! Why don't you grow up and admit that you were jealous of the love your father gave to a black woman instead of to you?'

Bruce reacted instantly. He stood up, stared at his wife with face twisted in pain and agony, bordering on tears, yet hard with hate and rage. 'Damn you!' He cursed and strode toward the door.

'Where are you going?' Betty shouted when Bruce opened the door. 'You better find Sandra or don't come back here!' She burst into tears once more and rushed into the waiting arms of crying Mable.

'I am feeling a bit cold,' Sandra shivered. 'It's the wet clothes.'

'The weather is getting worse,' John observed. 'Please for my sake, darling, let me take you home. I feel responsible for all that has happened. I love you too much to let this go on further,' John pleaded.

Sandra hugged him once more. 'I guess you are right. In fact, you *are* right, John. I feel much better now, but it will be a long time before I can forgive my father for treating you this way.'

'You must admit, he is very protective,' John observed. 'After all, you are his only child. He has invested a lot of love in you. It is only natural that he would wish the best for you. Unfortunately, the best does not include a black lover,' John laughed.

'That's too bad,' Sandra kissed his lips. 'There is not much he can do about that. He will have to learn to accept it. My mother can, so why can't he?'

'Yes, your mother was very friendly,' John recalled. 'How could two such different people ever live together and produce such a wonderful and loving person like you, Sandra?'

'Because, deep down, my father is also a loving person,' Sandra explained. 'But twenty-five years ago he had an experience involving a black woman and his father which turned him against all blacks.'

John smiled as he let his imagination run wild. 'Did he catch them in bed?' John teased, but Sandra was staring at him curiously and he realised that he had stumbled on the truth.

'You knew all about it?' Sandra sat up.

'Are you serious? Is that what happened?' He sat up.

Sandra looked at John and smiled. 'You men are so sexually obsessed that you explain everything in these terms. But you are right this time. He was only twelve years old at the time, and has never been able to get over it.'

'Well, that explains it, I guess,' John considered. 'But twenty-five years ago? Hasn't your father grown enough to put this incident in proper perspective?'

'I guess not,' Sandra said dryly.

'Anyway, I think we should be going back before you catch a cold,' John urged. 'Besides, your mother is probably frantic over this, which she does not deserve.' He stood up.

They walked across the cricket field in the pouring rain, hand in hand. Suddenly, Sandra pulled her hand away and began to dance, jumping in the air like a ballerina, her shoes held high. Then she shouted, 'Catch me if you can!'

The race ended at the eastern gate of the Botanic Gardens. Sandra was laughing and panting when John finally caught up with her. 'Let's rest here a little while,' she breathed heavily. 'Oh, it's so wonderful to be in love,' she cried between gasps, then threw her weight against John who held her closely, bathing his face in her wet, golden hair.

Betty sat on the settee exactly where Bruce sat last. Her tear-stained face was turned towards the door, waiting and hoping for the return of Sandra and Bruce.

Mable, on the other hand, sat by the kitchen window with

[152]

eyes peering at the access road to Knowles Gardens. She squinted through the pouring rain when she thought she saw someone approaching. She was right this time. She rushed to the living room to Betty. 'Dey comin', mam!' she announced excitedly.

They both hurried back to the window to see Sandra and John walking slowly to the house.

'I tell you he's a good man,' Mable cried, raising her hands in the air. 'He bringin' back Miss Sandra.'

'Thank God!' Betty cried and scampered to the door to greet them. Sandra entered alone. 'Good grief, child, hurry up and change these wet clothes.' Betty touched her joyfully. 'Where is John? Wasn't he with you? John!' Betty looked out to see John halt in his tracks. 'Come here, John,' she called, 'come out of the rain.'

Mable looked at John strangely. 'You Miss Flora chil'?' She asked.

'Yes, mam,' John replied, shivering in his wet clothes.

'Will you look after him please, Mable. I must go and attend to Sandra. She must be cold and hungry.' Betty hastened to her daughter's bedroom.

'Come, let me dry your shirt,' Mable led John to the kitchen.

'It's okay, mam,' John replied, shyly and afraid. 'I don't live too far from here.'

'But you waitin' for Miss Sandra before you go?' Mable suggested, smiling at John as he sat at the kitchen table.

He smiled back, feeling entrapped in an impossible situation. On the one hand, Sandra's mother and the housekeeper were imploring him to stay, while, on the other hand, her father had made it clear he was not welcome in this house. Suddenly, John got up, saying, 'I must go, it's past curfew.' He excused himself and hurried to the door. It was fear of Bruce Knowles, fear of those stern words of hatred and rejection that impelled him to leave. To be welcomed in the home of his beloved Sandra would be a great honour. However, if her father made this impossible, it didn't matter, since he could not change Sandra's love for him. That much John was certain of. That is why he walked briskly in the rain, happy, carefree, and very much in love.

[153]

*   *   *

The raging river was dark with debris from the mountains. Uprooted trees and rocks of all kinds tumbled along in cataclysmic disarray. Bruce looked on at the ravaging torrent, unmindful of the blistering rain, the clattering thunder and forked lightning.

He sat on the water pipe which had been his favourite spot during his youth. It was here he found peace and solace when he needed time to himself. He would gaze upon the flowing water and imagine the world to be a beautiful place without heartache or pain. But now he sat huddled, his arms around his knees. Betty's words kept ringing in his ears, 'bigot', 'jealous', 'you are the problem', 'you are jealous of your father's love for a black woman', 'why don't you grow up?' 'Grow up!' 'Grow up!' 'Grow up!'

Bruce bent his head between his knees in mental agony. 'What have I done wrong to deserve this from the ones I love?' Bruce murmured to himself. 'I have loved them and cared for them, and now they reject me because I try to protect my Sandra! Is that wrong?' He shouted to the muddy river. 'Bigot, my wife called me a bigot,' Bruce spat out. 'This is the gratitude I get from the one who promised to share my life till death.' Bruce nodded. 'Well, maybe I am, so what of it?' He shouted, standing up to address the thundering heavens.

'Brucie!' The voice was faint, but clear, beneath the echoing peal of thunder. Bruce froze with head looking up to the skies. 'Brucie!' The voice called again, and this time Bruce felt a sharp pain pierce his stomach. He turned quickly to see the dark shadow of a woman dressed in long cape and rain hat. Her hands were stretched out to him, and briefly, he imagined it to be his mother's ghost. 'Come, Brucie, let's go home.' Only then did he recognise the soothing, creole voice of Mable Prince.

'Mabes, is that you?' He cried.

'Yes, Brucie, is me. I come to take you home. Miss Sandra and Miss Betty waitin' for you,' Mable held out her hand as Bruce stepped down from the water pipe.

Bruce took her hand and drew Mable close to him. They hugged for a while, then he looked Mable straight in the eye and asked, 'What's wrong with me, Mabes? Why can't I accept all black people the way I accept you?'

Mable's glistening white teeth shone in the darkness when she spoke. 'For de same reason I don' accep' all white people like I accep' you, Brucie,' she continued to smile.

Bruce stepped back a bit, 'I had no idea you didn't like white people, Mable.'

'Dat is not what I sayin', Brucie,' Mable corrected. 'I like white people, but, I accep' you, an' Miss Sandra, an' Miss Betty more dan all de odders.'

Bruce looked at the affable black woman, and noticed the innocent glimmer in her eyes each time the lightning flashed.

'Let's sit down for a while, Mabes.' He took her hand and led her to the water pipe.

'You rem'ber de las' time we talk here, Brucie?' Mable asked fondly.

'Yes, I do,' Bruce replied, 'and it was a blessed day, twenty-five years ago. How could I ever forget, Mabes?'

Mable smiled, then her mood changed to bitterness as she recalled the past. 'Dat bitch, Margaret, she hurt you bad,' she snarled.

'She is still hurting me, Mabes,' Bruce confessed, 'and she has been hurting me for the past twenty-five years. Not a day has gone by without my thinking of Margaret and my father. Every black person I met in England reminded me of her, and I hated them. I wanted nothing to do with them and kept my family from them because I did not trust them. I grew up hating black people because I did not trust them. Now, I have turned my family against me because of this hatred. Mabes, I know it is not right, but, I can't help it.'

'Praise de Lord!' Mable shouted. 'Is good you know why you hate us. Some white people don' even know why dey hate us.'

'I don't hate you, Mabes,' Bruce hastened to correct his implication.

'I know you don' hate me, Brucie, but you hate black people, an' I black,' Mable explained. 'So, I in it, but, I not in it.'

Bruce looked at Mable curiously and smiled. Then, he repeated,

'So, I in it, but, I not in it,' and began to laugh suddenly. 'Come, Mabes, let's go home,' he caressed her around her shoulders and carefully walked the muddy track back to the dirt road.

'What happen?' Mable was still confused by Bruce's sudden joy, which closely resembled the revelatory ecstasy of the Pentecostal fanatic.

'Mabes, once again you have made me see the light. Although I knew it all along, I would not accept it. Betty has said this in many ways, but I ignored her. But now you said it once and I listened. When you told me, "I in it, but I not in it", I realised that if I really hated black people the way I say, then I should hate you, Mabes. But the plain truth is I love you because you are you.'

Bruce and Mable strolled home hand in hand, guided by the intermittent flashes of lightning. The heavenly thunder was like music to their ears, while the rain poured down its baptismal blessings, cleansing Bruce, symbolically, of his deep-seated hatred and bitterness.

'Isn't it strange how we reject people without even knowing them?' Bruce was reflecting.

'Yes, Brucie,' Mable agreed.

'Take this boy, Sandra's friend, who was so kind as to see her home in the storm?'

'Mr John,' Mable filled in.

'I know absolutely nothing about him, yet I threw him out of my house.' Bruce sighed regretfully. 'He could be a very nice and respectable young man, even as loving as you, Mabes. Yet, I rejected him only because he is black.'

'He is a good man, Brucie, from a good family,' Mable confirmed. 'I know his fadder and modder well.'

As they approached the house, Bruce hesitated a while to ponder how he was going to explain his behaviour to the ones he loved most. Their love meant the world to him, far more than the hatred for blacks he harboured all these years. It was time now to face his bigotry head on, and for that he needed the love and support of his family. 'Go on in, Mabes. I'll come in shortly.'

[156]

He leaned against the garage, exhausted from share thinking. 'Dear God, give me strength,' he prayed.

He was there but for a short while when Betty came rushing to meet him outside. She embraced him in his wet clothes and kissed him hungrily, while Sandra looked on from the entrance. 'Come in, love,' Betty pulled him in. 'Take off those wet clothes before you catch a cold.'

He was astounded by the hearty welcome, even from his daughter whom he had hurt very deeply. They were behaving as though nothing had happened. 'Just a minute, just a minute,' he raised both hands. 'There is something I want to say.' The room was quiet, but for the rumblings of thunder in the distant sky. 'Please sit down, and you, too, Mabes,' he beckoned. 'First of all, let me say how sorry I am for bringing all this pain upon you, especially you, San. I had no right to, and certainly no reason to. For twenty-five years I have been a bigot,' he looked at Betty who lowered her head since she had accused him of such. 'Yes, Betty, you were right. I hated black people all these years because of what you also rightly called a childish jealousy.'

'But you were only a child.' Betty tried to ease his pain as her own tears began to crawl down her face.

'I know, love, I was vulnerable then, but I have grown up a long time ago, and there is no excuse. I tried to justify my jealousy by seeing what I believed I saw in Margaret in every black person.' He paused and turned to Mable. 'But Mabes, my rescuer in time of distress, she taught me something tonight which I hope I will remember in my future dealings with black people. She simply explained to me why I love her, even though she is black. She made the simple observation that if I hated black people then I hated her, but I do not. She shattered a myth I had built over the years that black people cannot be trusted. I held on to this myth to justify my anger and resentment at my father and Margaret for their indiscretion in the wake of my mother's death. I was wrong. I was wrong, too, Sandra, to have treated your friend John so cruelly. Please convey my apologies to him and let him know that he is welcome here any time.'

'Thank you, dad,' Sandra sprang to her feet to embrace her

father with tears in her eyes, tears of joy and forgiveness. Then she ran directly to the telephone.

Betty, too, was overcome with tears of joy and sorrow, and forgiveness. 'I'm sorry, love, to put you through all this misery, please forgive me.'

'No, I won't.' Bruce was emphatic. 'I am thanking you instead for being so candid with your feelings and opinions about me. Only you can call me a bigot and be right about it. I am grateful you had the courage to confront me, and I love you for that.' He kissed her wet cheeks, then they turned toward the bedroom.

Mable had left the scene surreptitiously. She had no stomach for sad occasions. Her face was still drenched with tears, but her lips wore a triumphant smile, as she resumed her preparation of the night snack. Her smile broadened when Sandra came up to her with open arms.